IMMORTAL HOUSE

A NIGHTMARISH TALE OF VAMPIRES AND REAL ESTATE

Elizabeth

WRITTEN BY
ELIZABETH GUIZZETTI

Edited by Joe Dacy
Cover and Interior Illustrations by Elizabeth Guizzetti

This is a work of fiction. Names, characters, businesses, places, events and incidents are products of the author's imagination or used in a fictitious manner. Any resemblance to actual persons, living or dead, or actual events is purely coincidental.

Printed in the United States of America

Paperback ISBN-13: 978-0-9995598-6-4
Ebook ISBN-13: 978-0-9995598-7-1

Library of Congress Control Number: 2018910200

DEDICATED TO
EVERYBODY WHO FEELS PARANOID OR ANXIOUS,
BECAUSE LIFE DIDN'T TURN OUT QUITE LIKE
YOU BELIEVED IT WOULD.

Note to Readers:

In Italian: Stregone (M), Strega (F), Stregoni (Plural) directly translated means witch doctor or sorcerer. However, it is also commonly used to mean vampire. Using the current methodology, I created the word Stegx for a single individual who is gender neutral or where the gender is unknown.

The horrors of Seattle's real estate market await.

FEBRUARY 3ʳᵈ

SUNSET 5:13 PM

Chapter 1
Strange Client

L AURENCE ROCH WORE FANGS, BUT HE WAS NOT the strangest client Sarah Martin ever had in her car. She was vaguely curious if the fangs were implants or the temporary glue-on kind, but not enough to ask. One might not even notice them, except Laurence unconsciously rubbed his tongue over his left canine as he read the listings she had printed.

By his retiring quietness and the number of geeky clubs in Seattle, she assumed he was a LARPer. Of course, it might be some kind of kink. If he got off pretending to be a vampire in a Seahawks hoodie, it was no concern of hers.

Laurence's blue shirt accentuated the veins under his pallid skin. His dark hair, though quite full and curly, appeared strangely monotone and without highlight. In their initial meeting, he had claimed "to suffer from intense polymorphic light eruptions," and was required to view homes after sunset, which was why they were starting their showings at 5:30 pm, rather than earlier in the afternoon. Sarah could believe he never went into the sun.

She had warned she might show him homes after sunset in February, or perhaps even March when the days were shorter, but once the sun set after eight, they wouldn't be able to extend it much more than that. And, by inconveniencing homeowners, they might miss quality properties within his budget. Though the city had a population of over 700,000 people, and the sprawling metropolitan area was over 3.8 million, Seattle was still a city that slept.

Her concerns made him more optimistic. He had replied: "Yes, I hope to find and close on a house quickly as my lease is up on April 1st. I really need a place for my studio."

A self-employed painter, Laurence recently exhibited in several shows, but most of his income came from painting book covers "the old-fashioned way." With the recent surge in independent authors catering to niche markets, the work was steady.

When he spoke about painting, he became animated, but he seemed reticent about personal matters. However, she also learned his husband recently passed away, and he'd lost his home. Sarah knew it was a bad habit, but these facts created a story in her head of a young man who had married a wealthy older man whose children inherited his property.

Laurence preferred a single-family residence with a basement but was looking to keep it under $500,000, so he didn't need a mortgage. He could go to $550,000 if need be, but she understood stretching his budget worried him. He was fine with a fixer-upper. Though financially times were good, he was apprehensive about having debt on top of the ever-rising property taxes. There was so little inventory in-city under $550,000, but Sarah was excited. She loved finding her clients the perfect home, almost as much as she loved earning her commissions.

"Some of these seem pretty far south." Laurence scanned the listings. His voice sounded nervous.

"Your budget goes farther in the south end than the north, so we'll start in Beacon Hill, head to the Central District, then southward tonight."

"Sounds good."

By the warble in his voice, Sarah could tell something didn't sound good.

"Is there a listing you don't want to see?"

Laurence held it. "This one in Georgetown."

"All right."

He looked visibly relieved.

Trying to keep Laurence comfortable, she asked, "What genres do you work in?"

"Whatever people want. Romance sells the best."

A dark flush spread over his ivory cheeks, and he dropped his eyes to the listings, then out the window. He seemed to have no need to fill the car with chatter. His stillness set her on edge, but, on the plus side, he bathed and wasn't trying to convince her about his political stance, dietary choices, or new-found religion.

Chapter 2
Definite Maybes

L AURENCE SCANNED THE WHITE 1910'S bungalow. He had to find a home; without a safe place to rest his head, a stregone might go insane. However, this "Beacon Hill Charming Craftsman" had no curb appeal.

The typical big porch was missing. In fact, no dominate features proclaimed the era. Two front windows glowed from Christmas lights that hadn't been taken down and the ceiling fixtures inside which had been left on in preparation for their arrival. His reborn vision exposed the peeling white paint and missing shingles on the roof which looked like one rainstorm from collapse. Still, two old spruce trees would cast shade in the afternoon, and a row of three-story modern townhouses stretched southbound down the street. Mornings might be an issue, but maybe some plantation shutters would add character and block the light.

"This one is a bit of a fixer-upper." Sarah walked up the concrete steps and opened the lockbox attached to a blasé porch.

Remaining on the front walk, Laurence watched her long black hair swing in perfect harmony with her steps to her midback. It shimmered in the darkness. He wondered how she kept it so smooth, but his Catholic, Venetian, Napoleonic era upbringing would not allow asking a lady such personal questions. He kept a respectful distance, not wanting to set off any prey instinct. Sarah seemed not to be the type of woman taken in by superstition, but even in the modern age, fear was an intense emotion.

He ignored the sweet sound of her beating heart and rich blood flowing under her delicate golden flesh. To fit in with the informality of his adopted city, Laurence wore jeans everywhere, clipped his hair short and filed his nails. Most never gave him a second thought while he considered if they were a meal. Sarah Martin was not a meal. She was his Realtor.

He surveyed the hillside to see the view as a human would, taking in the warm lights of the other homes. He smelled spice, cooked meat, vegetation, earth, and creosote. People, domesticated animals, feral wildlife, and insects clung to life on this hill. "It's a pretty view in its way."

"Yes, it is. Quiet," Sarah said. "And within walking distance of the Hilltop area, the light rail station, and Jefferson Park."

"I like the location, but the house doesn't do much for a first impression."

"Give it a chance," she said.

Fearful she might sense death in his cold white skin, he was careful not to brush against her as she held the door for him.

He appreciated the new world's openness and equality, but he was a man outside of time. Or a vampire outside of time, if one would use the prevailing word. He didn't like the words "vampire" or "vampiro" because of the negative stereotypes associated with them. He liked the Italian word "stregone" because, on its own, it held neither negative or positive connotations, and only *Twilight* devotees had any idea what it meant.

Most of what Americans knew about vampires was from Hollywood or fanciful novels, and most of it was ridiculous. Except for what wasn't: the immolating sun and need for a secure home. Laurence's basement apartment was nice, but it wasn't safe enough. He wasn't sleeping as deeply as a stregone should. He kept waking in the middle of the day, covered in bloody sweat, terrified someone would find him and drag him into the sun. He feared if he didn't find a house soon, the restless dreams might drive him insane.

A coat room opened into the living room which was currently dominated by a large screen TV and old recliner. A tired-looking sofa was against the wall. The room had been sloppily repainted white, but the old maroon color leaked through, giving a pinkish hue. The original "charm" might be seen if one looked hard enough to notice the hastily painted old moldings and coved ceilings.

"Here's the powder room. The main bathroom is upstairs between the two bedrooms."

As soon as Sarah opened the door to the powder room, Laurence's stomach bounced. He didn't need his heightened senses to smell and see the mold in each corner and the brown ring on the ceiling.

"Is that black mold?" he asked, agitated. Turning away, he muttered under his breath. "Damn, Rob, why'd you have to go? I'm no good at these decisions."

"I'm sorry for your loss." Sarah's face was set in practiced concern for her client, but there was no change in her pulse or true emotion emanating from her expression. She opened her purse and unwrapped a tissue from a small packet and handed it to him. The action was so automatic, he wondered how often her clients broke down.

The image of Rob's kind face rose in his mind and brought waves of throbbing, hollow pain and overwhelming dread. He couldn't cry in front of Sarah. Humans simply did not react well to blood dripping from one's eyes.

"Forgive me. Can I see 'the vintage kitchen,' please?" he asked using the words from the listing.

"Right over here."

Laurence watched plenty of HGTV. Mid-century modern was all the rage, but the 1950's kitchen and bathroom fixtures were one of the reasons this house was still on the market after a hundred days.

He must have frowned, because Sarah said, "While this space can use some aesthetic upgrades, the layout is quite usable."

"Do the appliances stay?"

Sarah reread the listing. "It doesn't say; I can double check."

Feeling the creep of sorrow, he said, "I like the layout. Is that the door to the basement?"

Sarah opened the door and flicked on a light switch exposing some rickety wooden steps; beyond that, only obscuring gloom. "I'll wait here while you look at the space. Take your time."

Laurence took the first step into the dim and brushed a sticky cobweb out of the way. Though he had better vision than a human, it wasn't so good he could see in complete darkness. He removed his iPhone from his pocket and turned on the flashlight.

"Want something brighter?" Sarah asked.

"Please."

Sarah reopened her bag and handed him a small LED flashlight which had a square of tightly clustered bulbs.

He took another step following the white beam, his hand on the loose rail. The smell of moldy wet concrete below reminded him of death. He shivered, clenched the handrail and took another step. Below was nothing more than a concrete structure holding up the house. He looked at the flooring joists. His heart broke. He took a deep breath. He hoped Sarah did not follow him, he couldn't allow her to see his bloody tears.

If I had only invested before I slept! Amazon, Microsoft are in my backyard ... and I wasted the opportunity. Now tech workers and investors are buying houses faster than any normal person can. If I had been awake when the real-estate bubble popped, I might've invested in cheaper housing. Of course, if I had been awake, I might have saved Rob.

Laurence's heart ached for his beautiful husband. He hated thinking about how Rob must have suffered, lying on the kitchen floor dying. *If I had been awake ... If I kept more friends ... If our relationship hadn't isolated us, someone would have checked. It's my fault he's dead.*

Fastidious as always, Rob decomposed on the kitchen floor until he was nothing more than a skeleton with only mild staining on the linoleum and cabinetry. However, since Rob — being dead and all — hadn't paid the property taxes, the old bungalow went into foreclosure and was sold to an investor whose screams had awakened Laurence from his languor.

Dark creeping horror overwhelmed him as memories of his dayterrors slithered into his mind. His resting place in Rob's bungalow was discovered, and he was roasted alive as they carried his corpse into the sunlight.

Or worse, enterprising humans bulldozed him deep into the earth. He would have awoken, trapped. Buried under a modern mixed-use apartment building's parking lot; unable to scratch his way out; screaming in never-ending thirst.

Another wave of excruciating, stomach-churning pain pulsed within his chest. He shook it off. "Neither happened. I escaped," he whispered.

He forced himself to remember how he found his phone lying dead beside his bed. He plugged it in and had no power. He waited in a closet for the sun to set and found a library where he plugged in his cell and used a computer to find a basement apartment. He had enough cash to serve his needs and two large bank accounts. He was safe for now. However, he must find a new house in a city of only 83 square miles of land nestled between a bay and two giant lakes which had grown by 100,000 people since he went to sleep.

A stregone needs a place to lay his head and if I don't find one, I'll go mad.

"Get a hold of yourself." He wiped his eyes with the tissue and the edge of his sleeves until he was sure no blood remained.

Climbing the stairs, he said, "The floor joists look strong, but somewhere in this house is a leak. Mold down there too."

"I have the name of a good remedial service," Sarah said.

"Well, this is a definite maybe," Laurence said.

O N THE DRIVE TO THE CENTRAL DISTRICT, Sarah said, "I've sold in this next building before. The HOA fees are quite reasonable. There's a one-bedroom on the ground floor for 360 and a two-bedroom on the third floor for 525."

Laurence grew more quiet and still. He wasn't reading the listings or looking out the window. His eyes on his shoes, he seemed to be thinking inward. He might be embarrassed if he broke down. He looked like he might cry again. Of course, he was bereft.

She readied her tissues, but he rubbed his arm. In the passing street light, she noticed the smear of what looked like blood on his edge of his shirt sleeve peeking from beneath his hoodie.

L IKE ROME AND JERUSALEM, SEATTLE IS SAID to lie on seven hills; though the city was built on many more. Laurence lived through the regrading which split a ridge and created the deep valley through which Sarah drove her car. They turned up Dearborn, and slowly climbed the next hill which brought them to the Central District — one of the oldest residential neighborhoods in the original city where old homes with large lots were quickly being developed into modern line houses with large windows and rooftop decks. The contemporary architecture seemed spare and out of place in the older neighborhood. Worse, they were over his modest budget. All new construction was.

They stopped at a condominium built in 2005.

"There is a secured entry, one parking spot in the garage, and a possible rental of a storage room. The HOA fees cover water, sewer, garbage collection, and the maintenance of the property. It's a great location to everything. There is a bus stop on the corner which services several bus lines. The rules are fairly common." She entered a code into the entry which made a loud beep as it unlocked. She held the door open. As he passed, he felt her wandering sense of fear.

He rubbed his tongue over his fangs; they were still retracted.

Once inside, Sarah opened a small cabinet where several lockboxes were hidden. They turned down a windowless hallway. She knocked on the door to a west-facing condo. The homeowner greeted them.

The condo had the simple design of the year it was built. Beige walls were broken up by thin door casing, two-inch baseboards over tan carpeting and tan vinyl. Laurence gasped at the wide-open caseless windows which lined the living room's west wall, covered only by sheer curtains. Though the sun was below the horizon, he instinctively sought places where it wouldn't reach him. "Am I allowed to change the window coverings?"

"As long as it's white from outside," the homeowner said with an edge to her voice.

He hoped he hadn't just insulted her. "Oh good. I work nights, so I was thinking something more like blackout curtains."

The homeowner nodded.

He knew he needed to shut up.

Sarah gestured towards the open kitchen space with stainless steel stove, fridge, and dishwasher. "All the appliances stay?"

"Yes. They work great," the homeowner said.

Laurence touched a maple-look cabinet and rested his

palm on the cool granite countertop. He loved the way granite felt under his hand. There wasn't a lot of kitchen space, but he didn't really need a kitchen, just a place to wash his brushes. It wasn't like he cooked.

He toured the apartment behind Sarah. The homeowner followed too closely behind him. He felt her eagerness, her fluttering heart, her clenching stomach, and a second heartbeat inside her womb.

The bedroom looked a little too small, and the wide-open west facing window had a cheap set of metal blinds.

"Would a king bed fit in here?"

"This is a queen," the homeowner said. She quickly chattered about how if he used only one nightstand instead of two, a king would definitely fit. Though the bedroom wasn't impressive, the connected closet was huge — almost nearly as wide as the bedroom. It had no windows.

"Mind if I measure your closet?" Laurence asked.

"Go ahead, but I made a copy of the floor plan. I grabbed extras when I bought the unit. I'm an original owner."

"Wow, thanks."

Maybe a heavy door on the closet wouldn't be a bad setup. If I covered the metal blinds with a barn door or interior shutters, no sunlight would reach this room which could be an art studio. I could sleep in the closet. Change the moldings and maybe brick that wall which adjoins my neighbors...

They returned to the living room. "So what do you think?" the homeowner asked.

"I like the layout. It's quieter than I expected," Laurence said.

"It's a quiet building."

"Why are you moving?"

"My fiancé's condo in Capitol Hill is bigger. We're starting a family."

"That's wonderful. Congratulations. Thanks for your time." He inclined his head at the homeowner. Walking out, he realized he should've waved like a normal human.

Sarah said her goodbye, but she didn't say anything to him as they left the apartment. They walked down the hall, and Sarah hit the up button. The elevator dinged. A couple with a small black dog walked out.

The humans nodded at them. The dog growled under his breath and yapped as he alternatively pulled and backed up on his leash to get his humans out the front door.

Laurence sensed Sarah's wandering apprehension again as they rode to the third floor. The door opened. *Damn!*

A woman with a bored expression and another dog waited for them to exit the elevator. This dog was so well trained, it only whined from its owner's side, but side-eyed Laurence nervously as they walked past.

Sarah didn't seem to notice. Or perhaps she was too polite to comment. It worried him he didn't know what she was thinking, but he was never educated in reading human minds.

The north-facing condo was more spacious than the one downstairs, but the spare original moldings, cheap doors, faux maple cabinets and gorgeous granite countertops were in this one too.

The bedroom was large enough for a king-sized bed but had a regular-sized closet. The second bedroom faced east. It was big enough for a studio. He smelled dogs on the carpet and had seen two dogs in the hall. Unlike their human counterparts, dogs were not tricked by hoodies and modern haircuts. They knew what he was. Still, he liked the cleanliness of the building and the idea of a move-in ready home.

"I think that third-floor condo is also a definite maybe."

"I'M GLAD YOU LIKED IT." SARAH'S HANDS trembled as she put the keys back in the lockbox closet. Both dogs they encountered had reacted badly to Laurence. One had been so terrified, it went a little crazy. *Dogs sense things that people don't.*

"How many pets do you think are in the building?" Laurence asked softly.

Crap, did he just read my mind? "Most buildings in Seattle are pretty pet-friendly."

He held the door open for her as she approached. She didn't want to put her back to him, but, unwilling to offend her client, she walked through. Her office calendar had Laurence's name on it. Everyone knew where she was.

"I didn't grow up with dogs, and I'm afraid of them if I'm honest," he said. "But if dogs are allowed, cats are probably allowed too?"

"In this building, I know they are." She unlocked the car doors and glanced over at the passenger side window. She saw the blue reflection from his hoodie sit back to get out of her way. According to several movies, vampires didn't have reflections. Laurence had a reflection.

"I like cats and thought I might get one once I'm settled," Laurence said.

What's wrong with me? Some people just aren't dog people! I've still found them homes. The dogs sensed Laurence's fear and freaked. I'm getting loopy.

I need coffee.

"Would you like a latte or something? There's a Starbucks just around the corner."

"Sure." Laurence pulled out his cell phone. "I've a free drink coming; allow me to treat you."

"No, let me. You're my client."

"Please, I insist. You're doing all this driving and using way more gas than the cost of a latte. I already ordered mine; what do you want?"

She conceded. "All right, a grande latte please."

"Hot?"

"Yes."

"Sure thing. I love online ordering. It's so convenient."

"Yeah, me too."

She pulled into the lighted parking lot and looked at the people lingering around. He hopped out of her car. No one reacted when he walked in to get the order. In the moments he was gone, Sarah checked her phone. A few new emails. She thought about texting her husband but decided she was being stupid. Due to their family calendar, he knew she was with a client and was capable of giving Laurence's information to the police, if necessary. She still shivered as Laurence opened the passenger door and handed her the latte.

His cup read Peppermint Mocha. She could smell the peppermint. She watched him swallow.

Laurence turned and gave her a confused look."Should I have them remake it?"

"My coffee is fine," Sarah said.

"I really love the Christmas menu, but the peppermint mochas are a good year-round option. Did you try the toasted white chocolate mocha last Christmas?" He glanced at her. "I mean holiday season. I love Christmas — especially American Christmas — and sometimes forget not everyone celebrates. Sorry."

"No need to apologize. My daughters are huge fans of Christmas and the toasted white mocha."

"It's different in Italy," Laurence said softly.

"Christmas or espresso?"

"Both."

"How long were you in Italy?"

"Sixteen Christmases altogether. Family lives there."

*If he was a vampire, he couldn't drink that. **No.** Vampires don't drink peppermint mochas, because vampires don't exist. Laurence is a LARPer. A well-traveled LARPer.*

"The next house is just down the way." Sarah took a sip of her latte. It tasted the way it always did. She hoped her fake enthusiasm would morph into real enthusiasm or at least sound like it. "It's detached, but also a condominium. The listing says 'sold as is,' but the pictures looked pretty cute."

They drove east on Jackson and turned south on Lake Washington Boulevard and into the Seward Park neighborhood though there was no view of the park from the small series of 1906 stucco and wood Tudor Revival cottages.

"Wow! It looks like a storybook," Laurence said.

The words described the cottage perfectly: the red roof tiles surrounded a single brick chimney, the triangular lines reached upward giving a greater scale to the house. Four tall, squared windows were set in symmetrical pairs on opposite sides of a red door. The house itself was surrounded by a well-kept garden, with delicate violas planted around the front path. The edges of a tiny lawn were surrounded by a stucco and iron wall with an iron gate. It was a storybook cottage.

As they moved inside, Laurence scratched his chin as he peered into the "spacious living area."

Sarah was disappointed too. She immediately knew he didn't like it by his lowered eyes, but honestly, it was simply a letdown. "Any house over 100 years old will have problems, but the listing mentions a modern kitchen and two bathrooms."

The great room had no separate dining area, and the "modern kitchen" in a corner was smaller than the one in the condo. The ceiling bowed in the center. Laurence reached up and pressed it.

It moved.

"What's upstairs?"

"I believe a converted attic space, which is the master suite."

Sarah found the correct door which led to a carpeted stairwell. Laurence climbed creaking carpeted stairs to the upper floor, she followed. The floorboards sloped inward.

Had someone removed a load-bearing wall in the

living area to create the great room?

She noticed scorch marks around an outlet, but before she said anything, Laurence said, "From the outside, it looks picture perfect, but inside, I don't know; it seems like a different house, if that makes sense ... and I think one of its renovations didn't go well."

"I agree. I know you're willing to do some repairs, but that concerns me," Sarah pointed out the outlet. "As does the floor you're standing on."

"What's next?" Laurence asked.

Chapter 3
No luck

HOUSE HUNTING WASN'T AS FUN AS HGTV MADE it out to be. After viewing several more houses with Sarah, Laurence was tired and frustrated with the lack of possibilities. He wanted nothing more to lie in his bed with a handsome man or woman who didn't mind letting him have a sip of sweet, rich blood now and again. If he went to bed, he'd go alone with an aching thirst. He needed to hunt, and he needed to work.

"Hi, Larry," his wizened landlady said from the porch, her nightly joint in hand. She was the only person who ever called him Larry. She'd said it the first time they met, and her voice was soft and sweet and reminded of his mother calling him "Patatino" two centuries prior. (Little Potato is a common endearment in Italy.)

Betty's every breath was followed by a soft wheezing moan deep within her lungs. She only had a year or two of life left. The marijuana was for the pain. He would miss her when she was gone, but he would continue as he always had.

"Hey, Betty," he replied, ignoring the weed-stank.

"Any luck?" she asked.

"Nothing spoke to me yet." Laurence sat beside her on the porch for a few moments as he often did each evening. "The best house I saw was the first house I saw. I looked at some condos, but I'm not sure about the noise when I try to sleep during the day."

"Finding a home takes time. Coming in or going out?"

"Only to change. There's a Drink and Draw in Pioneer Square."

"Good. Stay busy. After Jon died, only by staying busy

did I function at all." She hugged him with the arm that didn't hold her joint.

He clumsily hugged her back, wondering if she would embrace him if she knew his true nature.

"You look too pale. Eating enough?"

Betty, like most of Seattle's residents, were most often more concerned that his pale, gray pallor meant he'd follow his beloved to the grave, rather than vampirism or even drug abuse. He didn't try to dissuade her of that idea.

"The bar has tacos," Laurence said.

"I suppose you'll be walking. Fresh air and exercise will do you good. Get your creative juices flowing."

"I'm sure it will."

"But if you get wasted, don't be afraid to call. I'll come get you," she said as she always did. She was afraid he might be mugged, or worse, walking up Yesler Way so late.

Laurence assured her he would, but knew he wouldn't. He never did. Even if she wasn't smoking, he wasn't sure the last time she drove her car. She had groceries delivered and used Metro Access for her doctors' appointments and visits to the Senior Center where she played bridge with her less-mobile friends.

He walked around to the east of the house and down the steps to the private entry of his basement apartment. He removed his hoodie and realized how much blood, his tears spilled on his shirt sleeve. He soaked his shirt in hydrogen peroxide before tossing it in the washer. He changed clothes and gathered necessities for the rest of the night.

He waved once more to Betty and walked up the hill, then down another towards the familiar streets emblazoned with Manga and Dragons and then to the historic Pioneer Square.

The dive had cheap drinks and cheap food, the perfect place for a Drink and Draw. He had told Betty the truth; the bar did have tacos. He did not order any. Laurence ordered a red from an undead-friendly bartender who slipped a few drops of blood into his wine. Some artists focused more on the drinking, some shared a plate of greasy nachos, some sketched, others wanted to network. The latter was his least favorite type of human as they tended to get too close to him when they saw what they referred to as talent. They always started to namedrop.

He said hi to a few humans with whom he was acquainted, introduced himself to a few others and pulled out his sketchpad. He drew the barman, the view outside the window and a cute redhead woman who blew a kiss at him. The redhead had such beautiful features she deserved to be immortalized in paint. He began drawing her in a classical pose, but with modern accouterments, nursing his blood and wine until the end of the session.

Laurence left the bar hungry. Between the hour and winter drizzle, the streets were mostly empty. He sought a quiet alley where the homeless dozed in tents. Listening to heartbeats, he found a man who slept alone. He smelled his flesh and tried to detect illness.

Human ailments could no longer harm him, but if he was infected, he might endanger a future lover. Perhaps that woman in the bar, if she was interested.

Silently, he sank his teeth into the man's wrist and drank until the man's heart slowed. He sliced open the man's wrists to camouflage the bite marks letting the final drops mix with the rain. He watched the fading light of his victim until the body was nothing more than a corpse. He dug through the man's spare belongings searching for loose cash. It would most likely be reported as another suicide.

Satiated, he ascended Yesler and turned onto First Hill. Some of the old houses were the same, many others had been torn down for mixed-use condominiums or modern row houses.

He glanced behind his shoulder and climbed the newly-erected fence. Rob's old bungalow was demolished as were the three houses next to it. However, the earth still held the memories. With a small garden spade, he filled a jar of soft soil from deep in the ground. This was the home Rob made for him.

Not wanting to ever forget his love, he filled seven more. Wrapping each glass jar with a dishtowel, he put them in an old backpack beside his sketchbook.

He would be smarter this time. He would buy a house in his own name. Then he'd invest small amounts in technology companies. If he was wise and cautious, compound interest might be the best friend of the stregone.

Chapter 4
Laurence's 1st Home

DAWN'S LIGHT HADN'T BLUSHED THE SKY, AND Betty's first floor was dark when Laurence arrived home. Careful not to disturb her, he entered his apartment. He wrapped each jar in tissue paper and used a dish pack to separate them.

He studied his sketches of the redhead. Painting seemed too difficult for such an ephemeral memory of a girl he didn't know. It was only an hour before dawn. Maybe he'd skip work tonight. From between the walls, he listened to Betty's slow thready heartbeat. All life was finite — except, he presumed, for a stregx.

Lacking passion or inspiration, he forced himself to stretch and gesso the canvas. He studied his sketch. He blocked out the composition until the first layer of paint coated his canvas. The gossamer red hair already taking shape as were her peachy reclining curves.

I should've planned ahead and asked the woman to sign a model release. Hopefully, the bartender would know how to find her.

He washed his brushes and allowed himself to be taken away with the image of Rob he'd refused earlier. He didn't know if he would ever love again. He didn't know if he could ever trust a person again with the knowledge that Laurence Roch was born Lorenzo DaRocco of Venice the first time in 1802.

It was so excruciating to remember his latest love, so he retreated to an earlier past, only less painful due to the passage of time. He turned on *Twelve Concerti Grossi* by Arcangelo Corelli to hear the music of his youth. The city's rats scurried around the garden outside. He almost matched their ephemeral beating hearts to the tempo. He removed the oldest jar of dirt from his box. This dirt had been turned to mud so many times it clumped together, but it held the memories of the last years of his human life, the first years as a stregone, and his first love. Laurence wanted to remember Suzan in the quixotic way that modern romances were told, but an orphaned daughter of a French trapper and an indigenous woman was, above all, practical.

L ORENZO WAS THE FIFTH-BORN SON OF A landed merchant who ensured the family's survival during the political upheaval of the Napoleonic era by trading favors or lending money. Lorenzo never considered the family estate his home. It was just the building in which he was born and where spent the first sixteen years of his life.

Napoleon created the Kingdom of Italy. His family's money withered away as Austrians scurried out of Venice leaving debts unpaid. As their fortune declined, so did his beloved mother's health.

On the last day of her life, his mother was surrounded by her children, daughters-in-law, and grandchildren. She bestowed gifts on each of them with the little wealth left from her dowry. He didn't remember what she gave the others, but she bequeathed Laurence a silver ring which he still wore to this day. Her pearl rosary was gifted to Caterina, the youngest and only daughter.

Laurence remembered it well because after his mother breathed her last breath, his father ripped that rosary from his sister's hands and informed her: "A convent is a better business than hoping you're kidnapped. I found one in the country which does not require a dowry payment. Pack."

"Rosa, see that she doesn't leave the house in that silk

either. Such wealth is wasted on a nun."

His eldest brother's wife, Rosa wept and gathered her two small daughters in her arms and obeyed. Everyone did. Except Lorenzo, who shouted, "You're a landed peasant."

After a vicious row in which nothing was changed or accomplished, Lorenzo left the estate with red welts lining his back and a broken finger where his father had failed to recapture his ring.

He lied about his age to a magistrate. Then he found a merchant ship and indentured himself to the captain, an American man with a weathered, mahogany face. Laurence signed his slip as a weak, untrained seaman whom the captain's wife shaped into an able-bodied sailor. She understood the sails, was a fine cook, and a better teacher. She showed her husband Lorenzo's fine handwriting and sketching ability and encouraged Lorenzo to learn English so he would be even more useful. His indenture slip was never resold.

Most were not so lucky.

At twenty-two, Lorenzo DaRocco entered New York State, a free man with $100 and a letter of recommendation. Wanting to assimilate as quickly as possible, Lorenzo changed his name on his church records to Laurence Roch as his former mistress suggested.

He found a job as a clerk in the Hudson's Bay Company. His shoulders grew tight hunched over a desk for twelve hours a day, but he enjoyed it well enough. He made friends with other clerks in the bachelor's quarters and sent his sister a little money for her comfort. He was happy to learn Caterina had found contentment.

Frequently, she wrote stories about making jam, bee-keeping, and caring for orphans who often came to the nunnery sick and malnourished.

Laurence was satisfied until a letter written with a trembling hand informed him Caterina had died of cholera. The rest of the bachelor's quarters faded far away from him as Laurence grieved for his sister. The loss of his mother struck his heart. The rage for his father and brothers evaporated.

One of the clerks, John Wallis, whispered, "Is all well?"

"My sister..." Laurence handed him the letter.

"I can't read it."

Another clerk, Tom Forbes, snatched it from John's hands: "It's in Spanish. It says his sister died of cholera in a convent. I didn't know you were a Spaniard."

"Venetian. Italian. Excuse me, I must write to my father..." Tears streamed down his face; he broke away and penned a letter.

John set a mug of beer in front of him but otherwise left him alone. All the bachelor's quarters knew of his sorrow. There was no privacy in communal living.

Laurence apologized to his father for his arrogance and willfulness. He spoke of his sorrow for Caterina then told tales of his good fortune. He asked if his father and brothers would like to come to America where many opportunities existed.

At the end of his letter, he signed Lorenzo.

Chewing on his quill, Laurence reconsidered. His father and brothers would not assimilate. His father's insistence on holding onto the disappearing feudal system was why Caterina was dead.

He burnt the letter in a candle flame. *If I'm to see Father again, I must be as a wealthy man with an industrious American wife, children and a governess to mind them.*

He penned a much shorter letter.

To my Brother's Wife Rosa,

The convent where Father sent Caterina informed me with great sorrow of her illness and demise. This news brings me distress as I have been sending a share of my good fortune for her comfort. Now I'll hold these funds in a trust at Monte dei Paschi di Siena for my nieces' dowry, so they do not share my poor sister's fate.

*When I left there was little Rosa and Maria,
if you please, send me any other names of my
brothers' daughters born in the years in which we
were parted.*

Lorenzo DaRocco

Tom touched his hand. "I suppose you and your father don't get on much?"

"No, we don't." Laurence met his eyes. Tom had read the letters over his shoulder and had the gist of it, but he was a good fellow and didn't speak it.

"What was the sister's name?" John asked.

"Cate," Tom said.

"Then we'll drink to Miss Cate's memory tonight."

"She was a nun-in-training," Lorenzo said.

"All that means is your stories will be filled with sweetness. Unless perhaps, you want to pray for your sister's memory instead?" John said with a wink.

"Drinking will be fine."

Even after nursing a long hangover with the lads, the thought of becoming a wealthy man lingered on Laurence's mind. He set aside part of his pay, not only for his nieces but also for the future Mistress Roch. He volunteered to travel to Fort Vancouver which offered a chance for even greater advancement.

THE TRAIN RIDE ACROSS THE CONTINENT WAS cold and uncomfortable, but no more than his time at sea. In the windswept Great Plains, the train made a water stop which changed him forever.

Hungry, he hurried to get a meal when something white dancing over the never-ending grasses caught his attention. A strange unearthly voice called. With only twenty minutes before the train moved on, Laurence purchased his supper.

Taking his place on the train's hard wooden seat, he couldn't shake the icy, uneasy feeling of being watched. The only people around were other passengers heading west, eating their own dinners, or tucking in for the night. He choked down a less-than-satisfactory meal of greasy sausage, beans, and coffee, wrapped his coat close to his chest and closed his eyes.

He awoke, unable to breathe.

Flowing white wiry hair strangled him. A white face stared at him. Her iridescent eyes met his own. Her hands found their way beneath his coat; the strega kissed him. Her tongue entered his mouth. He bit down and tasted blood as he choked.

She shrieked. Scarlet dribbled down her chin. She sunk her teeth into his wrist. The world spun in front of his eyes as her hair constricted around his throat.

The strega disappeared. A rotund man from China with calloused hands helped him to his feet and patted his back.

"Dov'e lei?. . . I mean, where is she?" Laurence cried.

"Who?" The man said.

Laurence couldn't explain in English. The strega was a myth, a fairy tale. "A woman ... was choking me."

"I didn't see a woman choking you," the man said. "You had a bad dream or perhaps a good dream?" He laughed.

Laurence did his best to laugh with him, though he was still shaken.

"Give him this." A woman with a tanned careworn face poured a shot of whiskey. "Just a nightmare, young man. A nightmare. Probably spoiled beans," she said. "You boys ought not to eat at the water stops."

The large man agreed. "Listen to the woman's wise counsel."

Laurence apologized profusely. The man sat beside

him and introduced himself as Li Wei, a translator for the railroads. Like Laurence, he left his home as a young man to make his fortune. "Eventually, I hope to send for my wife; she cooks much better than the water stops."

The two spoke late into the night until Laurence's fear and embarrassment subsided. Eventually, they fell asleep beside each other.

They awoke when the trained stopped.

A sheriff boarded a first-class cabin. Two men carried a sheet-covered stretcher.

The careworn woman asked the conductor, "What happened?"

"A man died in first class. Looks like a heart attack."

Other passengers whispered about the young man with prophetic dreams. Families stayed away. The older woman tapped her forehead and pointed at him.

Laurence's conversations with Li Wei grew stilted. Still, he remained beside him, and they spoke the miles away. When his own stop came, he hurried off the train and waved goodbye. Li promised to write but never did.

At Fort Vancouver, the strangeness of his trip was quickly forgotten. Laurence enjoyed the work, the daily company meals, and the fellowship he found on Sundays at church, and the company of the other clerks. They were much like the friends he left behind in New York whom he wrote often.

However, a month after he arrived, the sun began to irritate his eyes. Irritation developed into burning which eventually was so intense it felt as if two nails fresh from the blacksmith had been plunged into his eyes. He requested a desk away from the window.

Bread became distasteful. He ingested only meat, pushing a random potato around his plate pretending to eat.

He struggled to sleep and paced the bachelor's house at night which annoyed the other gentlemen in residence. He fought to remain awake during the day. His work suffered.

Head Clerk Taylor ordered a visit to the Fort Surgeon.

The doctor was a soft-spoken fellow whose wife could be heard in the next room with Mrs. Taylor. Though in the present day there would be privacy laws to protect him, at that time, there was none. Imagining the women listening in the other room as he stood naked in front of the men, Laurence found the non-stop descriptions humiliating. (Looking back, however, he knew his good fortune was with him. If they had any idea what he had become, they would have shot him on the spot.)

"Observation of your blood reveals nothing far out of the ordinary. Your heart beats slower than average but is steady. Speech is full and normal. The movements of your chest are full. No swelling of the liver or legs. No skin discoloration or abnormalities around his glands. No lice or ticks or other parasites found," Doc said.

"It's not cholera?" Laurence asked.

"What makes you think that?"

"My sister died of cholera."

"You were there?"

"No, I was informed by letter."

"Then, no," Doc said firmly.

"So, what's wrong with him?" Head Clerk Taylor growled.

"You spent many years at sea? Yes?"

"Six."

"Your history said you are of Italian descent?"

"Venetian."

"Hmm. My opinion is my patient clearly suffers from a form of anemia which is why he craves meat. In all probability, his deficiency was brought on by a sailor's diet and exasperated by the travel over land.

"There is plenty of meat to go around, I suggest letting Mr. Roch eat his fill so he might continue his duties. I also suggest his vegetables are mashed as one would give an infant to aid in digestion which should also help him sleep."

Then Doc got going: "His eyes are burning because he's not sleeping. He's not sleeping because he grew up on the coast, then spent six years at sea. I will prescribe a salt water wash for your eyes. Do this before bed and during dust storms..."

Doc cleared his throat. "Mr. Roch, during your period of indenture — how shall I say this? Were you in the care of a woman or, more to the point, did a woman care for you?"

Many European women sold themselves to escape brutal husbands only to be assigned a man because society deemed it unacceptable for a woman to live alone. Each baby lengthened their contract. "Captain and his missus didn't approve of such things. My mistress was the cook."

The doctor met eyes with Head Clerk Taylor then turned his gaze to Laurence. "And you weren't allowed to marry?"

"No. I was not allowed to leave the ship."

The doctor's eyes widened as if a new thought occurred to him. "And before that, your mother cared for your needs?"

"Yes. We had a few servants, but mostly my mother and sister."

"I see, then perhaps you'd do well to find a wife."

Laurence's accounts were not nearly big enough yet to have a wife. "A wife? But how would I keep her?" He did not say in luxury; the images in his mind were of horsehair sofas, carpets and painted walls.

"Create a budget, hire men to build you a cabin..."

Laurence did not want his bride stuck in a dirty cabin.

"Mr. Roch, while your work has been satisfactory, you ought to do a better job of being genial if you mean to continue to enjoy the luxuries of our community. Perhaps, the doctor is right. A wife is what you need."

"Yes, sir, I will find one," Laurence assured them. Even when the political upheaval shattered his human family's security, he couldn't remember being so frightened. There was nothing but wilderness around the fort. "How will I find a wife that my father would consider suitable?"

"What's suitable?"

"She'd need to be Catholic."

"I know a girl. She doesn't have much to recommend her though, but then neither do you." Head Clerk Taylor said, "However, you ought to know my wife is fond of her. And I'm fond of my wife."

"Who is she?" Laurence asked as he redressed.

"Suzan Davis."

The fort wasn't big, but twelve-hour days did not leave time for much socializing with the ladies. It took Laurence a moment to think of the girl. "Isn't she a bit young?"

"She's seventeen. If you wait, another fellow will scoop her up, just you watch. She already said no to two men, but they only offered her a country marriage."

Head Clerk Taylor invited him over for dinner where his wife —a sensible middle-aged French-born woman— grilled him about his past, Venice, his journey to the United States, and travel through the territories. She then introduced him to her good friend, Miss Davis.

Suzan had gone hungry too many times to have the youthful bloom of seventeen by the time she made her way to Fort Vancouver. She stood tall, the way an older, more mature woman would, neither flinching or flirting in Laurence's gaze. He was mesmerized by her frail beauty in a way that he had never been with any other.

Her father had her baptized Catholic. She spoke simply, but well. She did not read but was good with a gun. She came to the fort to sell trinkets and found a job as a seamstress for the wives and daughters.

Suzan thought Laurence too skinny.

"Fatten Mr. Roch to your liking," Mrs. Taylor said, "If you marry him, you will be a gentleman's wife and receive quality rations, but if you wait for the trappers to come in, you'll be one of the lonely widows waiting for her man, or traipsing around the countryside like your mother."

Suzan did not flinch physically, but Laurence saw her soul flinch as if Mrs. Taylor had struck her. "If I'm to be your wife, it must be official under your God. I won't be a country wife only to discover that you've another wife."

Mrs. Taylor asked him: "Were you promised to another?"

"No, Madam, I wasn't," Laurence said.

"Good. It's settled."

And they were married.

Suzan was everything a wife should be: thrifty, hardworking, and diligent in her care for him. He allowed, but also needed, her to run everything as she saw fit. With the household budget, she kept their small wooden cabin clean and bright and created wholesome, warm food. With her personal allowance, she kept chickens and rabbits in hutches attached to their home. He adored how she sang and stroked them when she fed them.

Laurence was shocked at how quickly advancement prospects reopened once he was a family man. He wrote to his father and brothers to flaunt his good fortune with a sketch of his new bride to boast of her beauty, and doubled the amount of money going into his nieces' trusts. Rosa wrote to him in thanks, and he introduced Suzan to her and the rest of the DaRoccos through letters.

Suzan did not fear his nightly wandering or his near constant need for meat. She never complained, but about two months into their marriage, the doctor still claimed he was anemic.

Suzan slaughtered one of her rabbits and collected its blood to make sausages which he ate with a ravenous hunger.

The rabbit blood running through his veins, Laurence felt satiated in a way he hadn't before. He watched as she painstakingly laced the rabbit skin into mittens. She was the most marvelous woman he had ever met. "You are the kindest wife a man could ask for, but are you happy?"

"I wouldn't have thought so, but an anemic husband

with a slightly nervous temperament and strange ailment is quite suitable for me." She sat on his lap and kissed him on the lips. "Will you promise me something?"

"What is that?"

"Don't drink your rum ration."

"Why?"

She repeated what he already knew: her father was a trapper who sold furs to Fort Astoria before it closed. Her mother was once a prominent native woman. Then her story continued, but in stilted whispers as if she was afraid to speak it. "My parents died from too much rum and debt which came from it. Let me sell your ration to other men who don't have families to care for. I don't know my mother's people. I might have been Métis, but my father refused. Now he's gone, and I was lost. I fear what it means for our children."

Laurence didn't understand; his knowledge of the natives was quite limited. Native women lived near the forts and often married white or Hawaiian men, sometimes in Catholic ceremonies, sometimes not. Their children were sometimes labeled Métis, sometimes not. Most spoke in a pidgin language which Suzan knew, but Laurence understood only the English and French words. All he understood was the depth of his wife's sorrow.

"You're Mistress Roch. I'm American, which makes you an American. Our children will be American." Seeing her concerns unabated, he added, "I will not drink a single drop. If you tell me to forsake the blood of Christ, I will do so."

She kissed him again. "Take communion as you seem at peace when you do. Besides the others watch. They whisper about you. Don't give them reason to hate us."

She was obviously afraid, but Laurence was still too sure of his own destiny to hear between her words. "Whatever I can do to please you, I will."

His purpose changed. He no longer cared what his father thought; all that mattered was Suzan. She was his muse and salvation. Someday he would build her a house with carpets, soft furniture, and painted walls. He would hire servants. He would become so rich, she would never fear her old life. Without understanding his malady, Laurence assumed he would leave her a widow financially and socially able to care for herself or remarry as she wished.

For two years, they lived in their cabin. Suzan quietly contented. Laurence planned for his next promotion, always in awe of his capable wife.

Old friends left the fort. New men came. The whispers about his strange illness and nightly wanderings grew louder, but Laurence didn't care. He worked hard in the office, he went to church and had another clerk and family over each Sunday. So what if the soldiers and workmen told outlandish stories about him? He was a gentleman.

Then during an unusually hot summer, several children perished.

Laurence thought he heard movement outside. Someone at the rabbit pens untwisting the wires. Clucking chickens. The footsteps of men.

He smelled pitch. Sparks fell through the ceiling.

Laurence pulled Suzan from bed as the roof collapsed. She screamed and coughed as Laurence dragged her through piles of falling wood. A soldier barred their escape through the door.

"Let us out!" Laurence screamed, trying to remain out of reach of the bayonet stabbing towards them.

Coughing, Suzan fell to her knees. Then the floor.

With strength he did not expect, he gathered Suzan into his arms and jumped from a shuttered window. They landed on the dry grass, embers sparking on their clothing. She wasn't breathing. He tried to revive her.

"Here, the monster is here!" A man shouted.

A bayonet sliced into his back. He screamed and jerked away from the agonizing pain. Somehow, he made it to his feet.

Soldiers chased him away from her, brandishing their

muskets and bayonets.

With men and dogs on his heels, he fled into the forest. Branches reached for him and scratched his face. He raced towards the salmon-filled streams where the women often fished. Eventually, he found himself in complete darkness with a singular fear of dawn.

He crawled into a narrow fissure between boulders where he knew the sun would not touch him and prayed Suzan had lived. Lonely terror took hold. When the sun rose, pain flared with an intensity unlike ever before. Every part of his being ached for an answer to this misery.

Dreaming to be reunited with Suzan in heaven, he followed the stream to the river and eventually to the Pacific where he tried to drown himself. He vomited up the seawater and knew a thirst more powerful than he ever had known. He tried to rinse his mouth in the fresh water of the river, but there wasn't enough water to quench his thirst.

Perhaps I am in Hell. If so, this isn't like I expected. Through beaches, through headlands, through primeval forests, he wandered, unsure he would ever be free of the horrible longing again. He hid from the sun during the day and hunted at night. When he was lucky, he ate the flesh of raw fish. When he wasn't as fortunate, he ate anything decaying. When hapless, he ate nothing.

One night, he found a trapper's fire. The meat smelled delicious, but the pounding of the trapper's robust pulse called. As if the devil took over his soul, Laurence ripped into the man's neck from behind. Gore poured into his mouth. The rhythm of the trapper's pulse and sweet blood became a balm. Laurence took his bloody heart as a snack for later.

More out of intuition than belief, he returned to Vancouver. He raced through the cabins and huts to the settlement's graveyard. He found two small slanted headstones beside each other. One read: Suzan Davis Roch, 1808-1827 Devoted wife and friend. The other was blank but smeared with chicken droppings.

He knelt in front of Suzan's stone. His prayers soon fell into remonstrations. "Damn you, God. You were supposed to take me! Suzan never did anything wrong."

He ate the trapper's heart and dreamed of the rich, strong blood of the fort's soldiers. If he could murder them all, he would. He silently moved towards the walls. When he arrived, a strange compulsion overwhelmed any thought of vengeance.

He stole a bucket and scooped handfuls of dirt from the foundation of his burnt hut. He grabbed clothes off a line and any other odd tools lying about that might be valuable or useful. An infant's wail and a single bell cut through the darkness. He dashed back into the forest and found the fissure where he first took shelter.

Clutching at his bucket of Earth, he dreamed of the moonlight on Suzan's hair and the loving way she kissed him. He was truly happy until he awoke on the cold, damp stones of his cave shelter with the thirst for blood raging through his body.

FEBRUARY 10TH

SUNSET 5:25

Chapter 5
South

"WE'RE GOING TO VIEW A TWO-STORY house in Columbia City and a mid-century rambler in Rainier Valley," Sarah said brightly to Laurence as he slipped into her car. "We'll head to West Seattle if you want to see more."

"Okay." Laurence kept his eyes on the printed listings and promised himself *I will find a house tonight! Then I can sleep.*

Since their last meeting, each day, he fought off sleep's terrors. He found himself trapped buried under mountains of concrete with painful thirst. Betty must have died in the night, he would think. He would scream, but no one would hear him.

He screamed so loud once that he awoke to Betty knocking on his door. He feared if he didn't find a house soon, the delusions might drive him insane—or he might lose control and hurt his landlady.

The two-story in Columbia City was only a few blocks from the major bus lines on Rainier Avenue. The wooden siding on the house's northeast corner crumbled and flaked off as soon as Laurence touched it. He exhaled.

She smelled must as soon as they stepped into the foyer filled with crumbling plaster.

"Woah. This is too much of a job for me," Laurence said. "We can leave."

They got back into the car.

She drove to Rainier Avenue, past Columbia City, past Rainier Beach.

Laurence ran his tongue over his fangs with more

frequency. His eyes grew brighter and flashed in the passing streetlights. He moved his hand to his jeans pocket, and she suddenly sensed something alien in his eyes.

An icy feeling went down her spine; she shuddered.

Laurence is not a vampire. I saw him drink a peppermint mocha! But what if Laurence believes he is a vampire? Ignoring the voice in her head, she drove on. She had a commission to think of. She shivered.

"Sarah, may I turn up the heat?" Laurence asked. "It's a rather cold evening."

"Go ahead."

She glanced at his hand as he reached for the heater. His nails were clipped short, and speckled with blue, green, and red paint. Not blood. Paint. *Good Grief, Sarah, that red on his shirt was paint!*

L AURENCE GREW MORE FRIGHTENED THE further south they traveled on Rainier Avenue. *Why hadn't I bought a bit of dirt to make me feel at ease?* Seeing Sarah's wide-eyed expression, he was terrified his fangs were expanding with the stress. He ran his tongue over his canine. It felt small in his mouth. *Dear God, don't let Sarah see my fangs.* "Are we still in Seattle?"

"We're within city limits, but, for shopping, you're closer to Renton. The reason I brought you here is this home is over $100,000 under budget." Her voice sounded smaller than it did previously.

He wiped his hands and noticed the twinge of blood stain on his jeans. He thought of the jars of old Earth packed neatly in his apartment. "Really? $100,000 less?"

"Your money goes further the farther south we go. We can even spread our search to Renton, if this house interests you."

"Think I could I live here without a car?"

"There are several buses into the city core within walking distance on Rainier. If we go closer to I-5, we have the light rail stations on MLK."

"I didn't realize how much further my money would go here. That's something to think about."

Her mouth set in a hard line, Sarah turned off the arterial and drove westward up a hill. They turned onto a quiet residential street with large quarter acre lots each with small ranch-style homes. She stopped in front of a mid-century brick rambler. It was as cute as the listing promised.

"The home was recently remodeled. Electrical updated, gas updated..." She opened the door and turned on the light. "The fireplace has a new insert, and these are brand-new laminate floors."

They toured the home. While the layout was good, his footfalls echoed off the dark fake hardwood. *Well, with this home so far under my budget I'll upgrade the finishes.*

They passed the kitchen which had a new, cheap laminate countertop, but with the old, repainted cabinets. "The kitchen has brand-new stainless appliances which all stay," Sarah said.

The cabinets were painted wood, he could have them stripped and refinished with stain. He could afford granite countertops.

"It has a large. fenced backyard."

He peeked out the sliding glass door. A rusted swing set sat in the north corner.

Neighborhood children might be loud when he tried to sleep. How would suburban life fit in with a stregone? It didn't fit with his second lover, Bill, who lived in the suburbs with his wife and children.

"Would it be inconsiderate if I walk around the block? I won't be long."

"Do whatever you need to do." She looked past him at his reflection in the sliding glass door. *Oh God, she did see something in the car. Think, think, think...* He moved away from the glass.

"Sarah, I'm sorry to bring this up. I don't know if it's improper..."

She stiffened.

"But can you tell me if there's a Catholic church within walking distance? I'm so uninformed about this part of the city. Maybe that should have been on my wish list."

She blushed and picked up her phone. Her smile returned. "I can let you know by the time you get back."

"Thanks."

She stifled a giggle as he left. Thanks to Hollywood, so many believed "vampires" were damned, letting people know he was Catholic was the easiest way to relax them. He didn't know what he had done to set off alarms, but he must be more careful.

All around him was quiet. He could see lights through the windows. Humans made dinner, watched television, played games. No one was on the street except a woman walking her dog who growled under its breath as they passed each other.

"Sorry." The woman quickened her footsteps. Laurence didn't look back, but he sensed when she did.

Seattle was no longer the port town of old. It was harder to find food that wouldn't be missed. A nosey neighbor could ruin it all. Hell, The Patriot Act could ruin it all.

The home was still in the city limits. The Sounder train or buses could get him into the city core. Further proximity from the bloodletting might ensure he would not be caught. But he might be visible to commuters. He'd definitely be visible to the bus and light rail drivers. If he wandered this neighborhood at night without a dog, he would eventually be noticed. *If I leave the city core, who knows if I'll ever afford getting back in. This cannot be an immortal house, I'm already thinking of trading up.*

He returned to the house.

"Well, I found St. Paul's on 57th," Sarah said. "It's about a mile away. Is that too far?"

"No, it's not too far. But this isn't it. The house is nice, but being here is weird. No one's on the street, and it's only seven. I enjoy Drink and Draws, life drawing classes, and other art meetups. I still go to bars with my friends."

Walking to her car, Sarah said, "There's still that listing in Georgetown if you want to see it tonight. Georgetown has an artist community. Or we could go to West Seattle."

Laurence's stomach dropped. "How close to the airport is it?"

Sarah showed him on a map on the printout.

Though he mentioned the airport, truthfully, he feared living too close to the Paper Flower Consortium which three old factory buildings converted into apartments as well as short-term housing for any of the undead passing through.

"All right. Let's go to Georgetown." Now, he really wished he had a bit of home in his pocket.

As Sarah drove through Georgetown, Laurence scanned for the undead. The Paper Flower Consortium was useful for updating personal information, remaining on the right side of accounting and legal issues, and had a well-known cleaning service. He was friendly with a few of the more normal folks.

However, too many fashioned themselves as Dracula, Lestat De Lioncourt, Louis De Point Du Lac, or even Lucien LaCroix. Except they weren't roguish rock stars, club owners or fallen warriors. Most were regular folks who happened to be reborn dead whether by choice or circumstance. The closer he got to Georgetown the more the coven would try to pull him into their lifestyle: a long mass and fellowship every Saturday night, wearing all black, keeping thralls. They'd ask him to get a sensible career and chastise him for watching football on Sundays. Not to mention the coffins.

The house was a small Craftsman with many period features, but the front yard was overgrown. The front door looked ready to fall off its hinges and was covered in graffiti. They walked around the yard. In the alley behind it, there was an RV.

"Uh oh. It looks like there might be squatters in there," Sarah said.

"Please, let's go," Laurence said. "I'm really freaked out. Sorry, I just don't like Georgetown.

"I don't want to waste any more time. I want that Beacon Hill fixer-upper. It'll be a lot of work to update the plumbing, but being here ... it helped me realize how much I want to stay in the city. In Beacon Hill, I'll still be in walking distance of my art meetups. I'm even sort of familiar with St. John's. Is it okay if I make an offer? Or should I go look at it again, just to be sure?"

SARAH DROVE LAURENCE TO HER OFFICE. *WHY did I let my imagination get the best of me?* Laurence was like every other shy, retiring nerd guy she'd ever sold a house too. This one pretended he was a vampire in his spare time, because in real life he was quiet, shy, and, artist or not, rather boring.

AFTER THE OFFER, LAURENCE FOUND HIS victim quickly and walked home whistling. He was in love with the house. He would transform something falling apart into an immortal just like him. An immortal house where he could rest his head forever.

He hurried up the steps where Betty smoked her nightly joint and sat beside her. "I put in an offer on a house in Beacon Hill."

"Wonderful!" Betty gave him a side hug.

"I can hardly believe what I'm doing. It's a bit of a fixer-upper. I could tell it needs some plumbing work, and I guess I'll see what they find at the inspection. They always find something."

She patted his leg. "Yes, they do. What's your plan for the night?"

"I'm staying in, I'm in the middle of working on a portrait. I can't wait to show you."

Chapter 6
Laurence's 2nd Home

LAURENCE READIED HIS PAINTS FOR THE glazing process. He would build layers of color to create a sense of depth and wonder. God, his model was beautiful. Painting her was a pleasure, and it kept his mind off Bill Caruso, his second love, his second home. However, his eyes kept slipping to the box filled with jars of old earth.

For nearly twenty years after his beloved Suzan's death, he wandered Oregon Country which became the Oregon Territory and then split to make smaller territories then states. As he had been, his victims were most often British or American men traveling alone and loose by drink. His clothing, dirty from mud and blood, rotted off his body.

He stole skins from a trapper to stay warm during the icy winters, but Laurence no longer cared about external beauty. He knew he had become a mythical monster.

He occasionally ran into sasquatches or werewolves who left him alone. Sometimes, he sensed a subtle presence which somehow, he knew to be a single or several stregoni. They, too, left him in peace.

However, some nights, Laurence missed companionship. He would seek fellow travelers. If they were kind enough to share their fire with a man who wore skins and carried a bucket of earth, he let them live.

Soon, every trapper welcomed him to his camp.

Laurence wondered why, until a child of five or six saw him lingering just outside the firelight. She called, "Are you the old man? Because you don't look old."

Laurence came closer. "What old man?"

"The old man who needs to warm his old bones."

Her brother, maybe a year or two older, came closer as the child cried, "It's the old man. It's the old man!"

"What old man?" Laurence asked again.

"All the old man wants is to warm his bones and have the smallest morsel of meat," the boy said. "If we give him these small kindnesses, the old man brings good fortune, if not, he's bound to eat us in punishment."

"May I share your fire?" Laurence asked their mother.

The woman let him into their circle quickly and gave him the first bite of meat from their dinner. He offered her a trinket he had stolen from his victims in payment. Once the children slept, she asked if he needed other comforts. Her mouth spoke of his pleasures, but sorrow-filled eyes informed him she was simply protecting her children.

He declined. "I wish for news. I've been in the wilderness too long."

He listened to tales of idiot settlers on the Duwamish River making pests of themselves as they cut down logs to build a city of wood: New York Alki. New York Someday. The first buildings were already swept away by the sea, so they were rebuilding. It was a fool's errand to build on a spit of land overlooking the bay.

Leaving the family in peace, Laurence headed north. He found the logging port of New York Alki or Duwamps, depending on who was asked, was now settled in a new location entirely.

Many people came through the port; if a few went missing, no one noticed. He drank from logger, sailor, trapper, and prostitute. He stole their valuables until he had enough for Laurence Roch to become a gentleman again.

He checked in with his accounts at Monte dei Paschi di Siena. The trust had been emptied, but his account was still there.

Under the name of Laurence Roch DaLorenzo, he wrote to Rosa informing his family that he and his father, Lorenzo, had been in the wilderness for some time. Lorenzo had been injured and no longer able to work, but Laurence was a gentleman of standing in their community. He wondered if Lorenzo's legacy had been well used?

A cautiously-worded reply came in the return post from his nephew. His father and brothers were dead. Rosa was a silly old nonna. The Lorenzo trust had been emptied long ago. Each of his nieces had married well, except one who used her dowry to secure her career in the convent. She became an abbess. The family's fortune was on the mend through an advantageous marriage, but there were many sons and not enough work. Were Lorenzo and Laurence seeking to sponsor a relative in America?

Laurence almost replied he would be happy to sponsor a cousin—then stopped to think. Lorenzo DaRocco was no more. The family he had known were dead. This cousin would be a stranger.

And Laurence had a stregone's thirst for blood.

IN HIS EARLY YEARS IN SEATTLE, HE BECAME vaguely aware of a stregoni coven called the Paper Flower Consortium, which settled in Georgetown during the 1890's. One young missionary asked if he'd like to visit and enjoy a Sabbath Service. When he declined, they left him alone but said he would always be welcome.

He attended human parties and enjoyed the frantic Bohemian lifestyle, posing as an artist. Taking a lover for a night at times; forgetting them as the sun rose. He occasionally sold a painting here or there, but most of his livelihood came from his victims. He showered in water that was always hot and washed his body with the finest soaps and cologne. He wore dapper suits. He slept on sheets of the smoothest cotton. Though he did not use china and silverware, he kept a set just for appearances. Yet, his true source of comfort was his bucket of earth from Fort Vancouver hidden under his bed.

By the 1920's, Laurence had rented a Bachelor's Apartment in the city's core. As the first wave of settlers flooded into the newly-formed residential neighborhoods, new immigrants moved into downtown. The hunting was fruitful. The sense of prosperity and optimism swept over America took residence in Laurence too.

He met Bill Caruso at a party. It was love at first drunken kiss.

They spent the night talking. Bill was the son of a berry farmer and worked his way through his engineering degree. He just missed World War I. He was fresh and clean like many young men who never saw an atrocity. He loved the American spirit and dreamed of future technologies. "All of humanity is going to fly," Bill said. They kissed again. Bill asked if Laurence wanted to spend the night with him.

He did.

Laurence was spectacularly happy as dawn blushed the sky. He rolled out of bed to dress and to escape the coming sun.

"Oh, you have a wife, too?" Bill asked.

"No ... wait ... you have a wife?" Laurence was crushed.

"Sure." He lit two cigarettes and handed one to Laurence.

Laurence briefly considered leaving a drained corpse on the bed as he took the cigarette. "I'm a widower, but I never was unfaithful when I was married."

"I'm not unfaithful. Dottie is the only woman I ever will touch again," Bill said. "As long as I keep her and the kids in comfort, she won't complain."

"Kids. too?"

"Yeah, two boys. Why does it matter?"

"I drink the blood of the wicked," Laurence said. "I'm trying to decide if I should drink yours."

"You're a vampire?"

"Yes, but please don't call me that."

"What would you prefer, Nosferatu?"

"I prefer stregone."

Laurence expected Bill to be frightened. Instead, he laughed and pulled at Laurence's waistband. "So you could kill me?"

"Well, probably. Yes."

"Take my blood. Make me yours. Then let's make love," Bill said.

Bill was taking the risk of mortal danger very well, but the sun was rising. Laurence had to get home.

"What? Are you sure? The sun … I won't be able to leave…"

"I'll rent the room another night, come here." Bill ripped off Laurence's shorts. At that point, Bill's intentions were clear. Thrilled beyond belief he might have found someone who might love him though he was a stregone, Laurence agreed.

For nights after Bill left his office, the men met in hotels and alleyways around the city. They played cat and mouse games where Laurence's prize was Bill's blood, or sometimes they hunted together. Bill grew excited by the kill and would always take Laurence someplace they could be alone.

One night, a pretty woman with blond shoulder-length hair confronted them in a dank alley as Bill was ripping Laurence's shirt open. All she said was, "Bill."

Laurence was shattered as he saw Dottie Caruso for the first time. The agony was written on her face. He had hurt this woman—not just some faceless, nameless wife. They had kids too.

Bill was enraged. "What are you doing here?"

"Asking for a divorce. Apparently following you into dark alleys is the only way I can see my husband."

"How…?" Bill said. His face turned various shades of red and purple.

"Bill, go home. Forget about our deal," Laurence said.

"Of course, there's a deal," Dottie said bitterly. "He

won't, Mister..."

"Laurence Roch."

"Mr. Roch, he's yours."

Bill pushed his wife into a wall. "Go home, we'll talk about this later."

"No! I want a divorce!"

Bill slapped her.

Sometimes in love-making, Bill slapped Laurence, but in his mind, what they did to each other didn't matter because they were approximately the same size and he agreed to it. However, when Bill slapped Dottie, Laurence saw every man who beat his wife — including his own father. He wanted to rip Bill to pieces. He did not. Instead, he grabbed Bill's arm and pulled him close "If you ever mistreat her again, I'll leave and take your family with me. I swear to all that is holy, you will never find me or them." He turned to Dottie and offered his assistance.

"Don't touch me, either of you," she cried.

"We won't, but we need to talk," Laurence said.

Dottie rose to her feet and walked into a nearby diner. They took a booth in the back. She listened to Bill's explanation and pleas quietly. Laurence was relieved Bill did not mention the details of their relationship.

"I need this. I swear to you, I'll never touch another woman, but I need this. I love you, Dottie; if I didn't, I wouldn't have hit you when you said you wanted a divorce."

She didn't answer him; she looked at Laurence. "Mr. Roch, I suppose you too have a family to neglect?"

"I'm a widower. My wife, Suzan, passed away several years ago."

"She must have been very young to have died several years ago."

"Nineteen."

"Childbirth?"

"Yes. Both Suzan and our child were lost." It seemed easiest to lie. And it was the right decision as her eyes softened.

Dottie didn't take her eyes off Laurence as she spoke to Bill. "It's bad enough I have to share you in the night, but I expect you to help me and be my husband and a father during the day. I expect you home on Sunday morning for church. And I expect you home on Thursday night for bridge."

"We'll do anything you want. I never meant to be a homewrecker," Laurence said.

"Bill's been kinder to me and the kids once he started coming home later." She welcomed Laurence into their suburban home for non-religious holidays: "As long as you keep your sins away from the children and our neighbors."

He should have run or told Dottie to run. She, who had bravely come looking for her husband, was only twenty-one and had two small boys who she thought needed their father. At that point, though Laurence had lived for nearly fifty years, he also didn't have enough experience with love to understand its destructive nature.

WITH NO LIES BETWEEN THEM, THE NEXT fifteen years were more exciting than any Laurence had ever lived then or since. However, when Bill turned thirty-five, something changed. He complained about the gray in Dottie's hair and the lines on her face which Laurence thought grew more delicate as she entered her mid-thirties.

For the next few years, he interrogated Laurence about his past, the train, and the strega who changed him in several different ways, altering the question ever so slightly. He watched films about the undead and read books on the occult.

Laurence didn't worry. Bill had everything. He survived into the Great Depression with his job intact. Dottie kept the house and volunteered in their church's soup kitchen. His older boy graduated high school, and his younger one was doing all right in his studies.

Then he asked Laurence to change him.

"I don't know how I became a stregone," Laurence admitted.

Bill questioned him again. Laurence answered truthfully and held onto the belief that if he could just get Bill passed this obsession, everything would return to the way it had been.

Their lovemaking became more violent and frenzied. Bill increased his studies into the occult. He drove to strange bookshops and sought underground clubs.

Until the night everything changed.

"I can't believe it," Bill said.

"What?" Laurence looked up from his book.

"It's in the directory!" Bill said, "I guess the yellow pages really can tell you everything."

"What are you talking about?"

"The Paper Flower Consortium. It's right here under Vampire Services!"

Laurence did not hide the shiver that ran up his spine by the mention of the coven.

"You knew there were other vampires in Seattle?" Bill accused.

"A missionary..." Laurence ducked as Bill hurled the phonebook at his head.

The book hit the wall and fell open onto the floor, spine cracked. The chair Bill had been sitting on screamed against the wooden floors. He stormed across the room. He grabbed Laurence's wrist and forced him to stand.

"Look at me!" Bill shouted. "Why should you be the only one to know the secrets of life and death?"

"But I don't know."

"You knew where to get the information. You played me." Bill slapped him.

This was no playful slap during lovemaking. Laurence

couldn't believe the anger behind it. And he knew if he hit back he might kill Bill.

"You have a family," Laurence stammered. "Bill Junior just entered the university, but Jason is still at home..."

"I'm leaving Dottie," Bill said.

"What? How could you leave Dottie?"

"What does that matter?"

"It matters if we hurt your family."

"We hurt them? For eighteen years, I suffered playing husband and father. When do I get something?"

"Do you know what I would have given to have had eighteen years with Suzan?" Laurence shouted. "Everything is perfect, and you're ruining it!"

Bill slapped him again. "Nothing is perfect! Oh, you get to play the magnanimous uncle, giving my sons toys and trips, treating Dottie to nights on the town. But I had the responsibility. I was the one who had to go home. To work. To bridge. What did you do? Pretend to be an artist? Pretend to be human?"

The third slap cut open Laurence's lip.

"I swear if you ever hit me again, I'll kill you," Laurence cried.

"Good. Do it. Put me out of my misery."

Laurence couldn't move. It would be so easy to tear Bill's throat, spill his blood. He crumpled onto his chair.

Bill's voice grew soft and gentle. "Take me to the Sabbath. Just one. If you hate it, you never have to go back."

LAURENCE ACCOMPANIED BILL TO A PAPER Flower Consortium's Sabbath. The service was similar to a regular Catholic service, but foreign somehow. Laurence watched the stregone in front of him and copied whatever he did, but spent most of the time confused and uncomfortable sitting on a wooden pew or genuflecting on the wooden riser, then realizing the service had moved on without him.

Laurence wasn't sure how he knew this, but most of the undead in attendance were a few centuries old, but there were two younger ones scattered about. The four seated in the front pew were primeval.

Like Seattle around them, while many were of European extraction, there were other nationalities represented as well, especially China and Japan. The humans, seated among them, were also from every race and creed. There were no children. Then he noticed many stregoni simply sat respectfully quiet instead of genuflecting.

He decided to take their example.

At the end of the service, the two ancient ones from Europe approached him. The female clasped his hands. "We are so happy you came to our Sabbath, Laurence. I am Agata. This is my husband, Jakub. We are originally from Moldovia; we understand you are from Venice?"

Agata looked to be a woman in her thirties, her long chestnut braids went past her waist. Jakub might be a bit older, but not by much. Looking at the Shakespearean beard and mustache and midback curls, Laurence was glad he wasn't stuck with that much hair for eternity.

"Bill wanted to come," he replied.

They nodded at Bill but did not touch him.

"Will you stay for our fellowship?" Jakub asked.

"Yes," Bill said. "We are staying."

Laurence didn't disagree, though he didn't want to stay. They were introduced to Kanae and Hitomi, two ancient vampires from Japan who toured the area as there were many settlers of Japanese descent in Seattle and Bellevue.

Laurence shook their hands and bowed at them. His mind spun, but he was most impressed that while stregas were stunning, there was a lack of delicacy and demureness. They met his eyes the way Suzan had met his eyes. They were hunters as he was a hunter.

"Some covens have a reputation for encouraging segregation, but as you see, we do not discriminate here by nationality, religion, or other social constructions," Jakub said. "You and your lover are safe here. Many people would like to meet you. Mingle."

He said his goodbyes to Kanae and Hitomi and overheard Jakub complain about: "Young vampires today ... how informally they dress."

"But that is the way the world," Hitomi answered him.

It was like a human party, except everyone wore black clothing of different, past eras, even the women. People laughed and drank wine mixed with blood. Laurence felt so under-dressed in his brown suit. Bill smiled and chatted with everyone.

He approached groups, but couldn't figure out how to break into their strange conversations. The humans in attendance served them graciously or seemed to be enchanted and would not speak to him.

"Oh, Laurence," Agata said. "This is my first born, Pascaline."

"Hello." Pascaline put out her hand.

He wasn't sure if he should shake it, kiss it, or kneel before her and promise to be her champion. She glanced at her "mother" and shook his hand. The touch was electric. He couldn't dare look away from the piercing hazel eyes. He wanted to kiss the freckles on her nose and run his fingers through her copper hair.

He spotted Bill behind her. He looked at his shoes, trying to think of something safe to say.

"It is nice to finally meet you," Pascaline said.

His shoes did not advise him on what to say. He said nothing. She turned away and spoke to someone else.

Agata handed him a cup. He could smell the blood over the sour raspberry notes in the wine. "Lost bunny, it's always hard to make new friends at parties. Your William seems to be having fun though."

"I'm sure he is," Laurence said.

Agata patted his shoulder and introduced him to another couple. Loretta Fabron, Agata's second born, and her husband, Charles, who was born of Jakub.

They were gracious. Charles was, notably, easy to speak to, as he too, once worked in the fur trade. He believed he was the luckiest man to have ever walked the Earth to catch such a prize as his lady, Loretta. They had been married for two centuries, hardly a quarrel between them.

Still, something about the old-fashioned mannerism's bothered Laurence. There was a new world, but these people knew nothing of it. Nor did they care.

He finally found Bill in the crowd. "I don't understand this place."

"What do you not understand?" Bill said, annoyed. "This party is darb."

(Darb: antiquated adjective meaning great or fun.)

"Why won't humans talk to me?"

Bill sighed. "Some humans are paid servants. Others are part of a 'program' and learning the ways of the vampire before they would be turned. Some are lovers."

"This is weird; can we go?" Laurence asked.

"In a minute. You're being a wet blanket."

He lost Bill again in the crowd. He tried to see their faces. Jakub was beside him, refilling his glass. "There's no need to hunt here."

"I-I wasn't. I can't find Bill."

"Ahh. Yes. Pascaline told me you're shy."

Jakub brought Laurence to Bill, who was in deep conversation with a blond stregone who wore a handlebar mustache.

Jakub introduced him. "This is Derrik Miller, so young he has two names just like you and Bill.

"Derrik, this is Laurence Roch."

A vague threat or rivalry originated from Derrik as the

men shook hands. Laurence wasn't sure why or even how he knew it was there. Maybe it was the way Bill looked at him. Maybe it was his fine mustache.

Derrik shook his hand. "Bill says he's not your pet or thrall."

"Thrall? I don't keep slaves."

"They aren't slaves; we keep no thrall who doesn't want to be a thrall," Jakub said.

Laurence backed away. "Bill, please, let's go."

"You're overreacting, getting caught up on the language," Bill said.

"Why did you come here?" Derrik pressed his wrist.

"Bill wanted to come and learn your ways."

"He wants to enter the program?"

"You'd have to ask him. Not me. I want nothing to do with you or your ways. I want to go home."

Derrik released him.

He was outside the factory. Alone. He waited, watching the moon set. He eventually walked to his apartment and went to bed. Alone.

The next dusk Laurence awoke with Bill on top of him.

"Drink of me and turn me into a vampire," he asked with a sultry whisper.

"I can't. I don't even know how."

"I know how." Bill punched him in the mouth. The shock was followed by throbbing pain. He leaned down; his tongue reached for his mouth.

Laurence pushed Bill off him and rolled to his feet. He clenched his fists and held himself still, fearing he might throw his lover through the wall.

Bill sobbed. "Three years, the program is three years. I'll be nearly forty-two. But you could change me now. We could be together forever ... why don't you want me anymore?"

"I still want you."

"Why won't you change me?"

Because deep in his heart, he feared what Bill might be

as a stregone. Laurence didn't answer.

"Change me, or I'm leaving."

"I can't change you. I can't. If I do it wrong, you'll die."

Bill slammed the door as he left.

Laurence knew where Bill was going, but he didn't stop him. He crossed town to the northern suburbs, slipped into Dottie's back garden and shoveled dirt into a jar.

FEBRUARY 11ᵀᴴ
SUNSET 5:26

Chapter 7
Disillusionment

LAURENCE PACED HIS BASEMENT APARTMENT, waiting for Sarah's call. He watched HGTV and planned all the exciting renovations he wanted to accomplish.

The day grew late. He needed sleep, Laurence lay in his comfortable bed, but sleep wouldn't come. He rose and paced. He slipped his hand in the small jar of old earth from Vancouver. It didn't help.

His phone buzzed. "Hi, Sarah!"

There was a pause. Two centuries of experience told him that was never good.

"I'm sorry, Laurence, but the seller accepted an over-asking price offer by an investor."

Throbbing, weak-in-the-knees disappointment disoriented Laurence. He wasn't sure what to say. Thank God for Miss Manners. Etiquette took over. "I'm sorry to hear that. Is there anything else on the market to look at?"

Sarah explained she would find more listings. They'd view more properties in two days. With each word, shivers shot through his body.

He hung up the phone. Disappointment morphed into anger. "I would have loved that house, made it new again, made it eternal."

The investor would kill it —tear it down and build a row of line houses. Wanting revenge for the next fallen building, Laurence craved rich blood. When the sun set, he would find it.

L AURENCE PACED PIONEER SQUARE. RELISHING the lingering excitement of the pursuit, he ignored the homeless on the corners, hipsters and sports fans heading to the stadiums. He wanted more in his victim. He wanted wealth. With every step, he imagined the taste of rich blood and flesh.

His subconscious warned him: *flesh will be messier and more expensive to clean.* He ignored his mind's hesitation. Tonight, he would fulfill all his desires.

He sought the newer, high-priced bars for well-dressed men and focused on shirt labels which screamed their expense.

A man left the bar in a button-down Hugo Boss shirt. His dark hair was shiny and well-kept, his muscle-bound flesh was darker than most. His eyes swam pleasantly, but his loping pace did not suggest drunkenness.

Laurence followed him into another club.

The bouncer scanned him and checked his state-issued ID.

"Don't drive?"

"Never saw the point in the city."

The bouncer made a noncommittal murmur and let him in.

The scent of warm, sweet blood and beating hearts danced. Dry, hoarse breaths followed the DJ's pounding rhythms. The smell of the sweating humans nearly overwhelmed Laurence. Their frenzied meat caught the dim flashing lights. He caught the exquisite profile of a golden-haired woman, a perfectly carved cameo. He wanted to bite into that perfect white flesh, but she ignored him as she sauntered to a table full of laughing women. His dark-haired prey came into focus. The pleasure of the hunt was maddening.

The man ordered a beer. Laurence ordered a red wine. Careful the bartender didn't see his focus on his prey, he checked him out through his glass. When it was empty, he ordered another. During the same time, the man ordered two more beers. His prey asked the bartender where the restroom was.

Laurence paid his tab.

The bathroom was only two stalls and a urinal. There wasn't a lock on the door. Damn.

The pounding reached a crescendo as he reached for the man's wrist.

"What do you want?" his victim said.

"Just you," Laurence replied.

The man's hands ran under his hoodie and t-shirt. Laurence grabbed his brawny shoulders and bit his neck. He loved a willing victim. Behind them, someone opened the bathroom door. Laurence was pretty sure the interloper didn't see anything but two men making love before he made a quick U-turn, swearing under his breath.

His prey pulled him into the last stall and pushed him against the damp cement wall. Laurence fell backward, smacking his head. The man was on top of him, kissing him. The stench of alcohol on his saliva and beating heart made Laurence growl. The man didn't even look surprised as Laurence's fangs expanded. Laurence bit again as the man fumbled with their clothing. His grasp grew weaker as he unzipped Laurence's jeans. Laurence's head spun from the alcohol-soaked blood. He moved to his prey's muscular neck, he tore the flesh. Blood bubbled and spilled from the open wound splattering Laurence's face and t-shirt. The chewing and sucking of the warm flesh and blood delighted him. His victim's heart slowed. His heart stopped. Laurence kept eating, gorging himself on his well-deserved meal.

Once he had his fill, Laurence dropped the man's corpse onto the toilet and snapped back to reality. How was he going to get this body out of the bathroom? Someone else more curious or the bouncer might come in! He couldn't leave a dead body in this bathroom; he would be seen!

What have I done? He turned around, tripped over his victim's long legs and sprawled onto the bathroom floor.

He rifled through the man's wallet. He kept the cash, then wondered what he should do. He was too drunk to plan. He only had one place to turn. He brought up the Paper Flower Consortium's new app on his iPhone.

The development team had done an admiral job. The app was simplistic in design — made for vampires drunk on their asses or terrified out of their minds. He hit the button for Norma's Cleaning Service. *Damn me. I shouldn't be spending money like this when I'm trying to buy a house! What was I thinking!*

He put his phone in his pocket, but sitting on the cold, damp floor, he rechecked the app again. Eleven minutes till arrival.

He willed it to go faster. The time jumped to five minutes.

Someone knocked on the door and peeked into the bathroom. The man entered the first and smaller stall and took a massive dump. Laurence listened to the flush, the slam of the stall door, and then the outer door. The guy didn't wash his hands.

He looked at his phone again. Two minutes.

Exactly one minute and 59 seconds later, the bathroom door opened again. Norma, a shorter than average strega even in the five-inch spike heels, arrived. Her wild dark curls spilled around her heavily made-up face like a halo and huge ivory breasts under a sparkling sequence top, entered the bathroom laughing. Followed by a silent white human male in his late thirties, whose thick muscles looked to be built of solid stone.

"Are you sober enough to walk?" Norma asked.

"Yes. I think so."

Norma didn't look like Norma. He wondered if she got

a boob job.

"Good. Do you have a tab?"

"No, I paid cash."

"Does he?"

"I don't know."

Norma quickly cleaned blood off his victim's face, covered the wound. She removed two tightly packed windbreakers from a small clutch. She slipped the maroon one over the dead man's bloody shirt and gave the black one to Laurence. She taped something onto the top of his victim's mouth. A man's drunken singing voice filled the bathroom.

"Put that on and sing," Norma said.

Laurence slipped the windbreaker over his hoodie. He sang badly, a few beats behind the song playing from the dead man's mouth. He didn't really know the words.

The massive human took hold of Laurence's arm. Together the three men stumbled out of the bathroom and ran into a man and woman dancing who said, "Hey!" as Laurence tried to apologize.

Norma pointed the victim out to the bartender. "Tab?"

The bartender showed her the bill. She paid in cash to cover his beers, took back his credit card and slipped it into the pocket of Laurence's victim. She waved at the bartender as they staggered out. They wandered to the next corner where a black van with a single red stripe waited.

The heavily-built human set the corpse on a sheet of plastic and ambled into the driver's seat without a word. Norma jumped inside and put her small white hand to help Laurence up and into a seat.

Once on the road, Norma rolled down her sparkling top and the false chest, then shimmied out of the pants, exposing a pink tank-top with a unicorn pooping a rainbow and jeans shorts. Her spiked heels were set in a little cubby and replaced with sneakers. Without her disguise, Norma was still Norma.

Laurence wouldn't judge Norma if she wanted to

modify her body, she was only a young teenager when her humanity was stolen from her. He was strangely relieved. He didn't want her to change.

"Laurence, I'm sorry about your husband."

By the look in her mournful eyes, he believed she meant it.

"Thanks." His mouth went dry. "Oh God, The Paper Flower Consortium set their eyes upon me again. You'd tell me right?"

"Sure, but..."

"Will they force me to follow their rules? How will they react if they discover I'm doing stupid things to men in bathrooms ... They might request I join the Consortium or leave Seattle. How could I be so stupid!"

"Hey, you called me, and I'm here now. The Consortium only wants you to take care of yourself. A fair number go to bars, you know. If they didn't, I'd be out of a job."

Laurence felt like vomiting, but he nodded.

Norma handed him a barf bag. "How's the house hunting?"

"I was outbid on a house I loved."

"He the guy who made the counter offer?"

"No, but he's the type who would. It's so hard to get a house with so many investors."

"I hear that. Did you know they say Seattle is the hottest market right now?" She shook her head at the corpse. "Blood is easier to clean than flesh."

"Investors stole Rob's house. I lost my temper. God, why did I do this?" He buried his face into his hands. "I dishonored Rob's memory. Why did I do it?"

"Because you're lonely," Norma said softly.

"God, why did Rob leave me?"

"I don't think he meant to," Norma said. "I'm sorry I didn't know what happened. If I had, I would've gotten you out without waking you from your torpor."

"It's my fault. I should've turned him," Laurence cried

into his hands. They turned bloody with his tears.

"Did Rob want that?"

"No," Laurence said.

"Listen carefully."

"Yes?"

"Next time eat a raw steak with cow's blood. It's cheaper. And you won't be weeping in my van. You always hate yourself when you act impulsively. What can you tell me about your victim?"

"I met him in a bar. We made out in the bathroom." He shouldn't say these things to a woman — especially this one who was so much younger than he and whom he once taught math and accounting principles. He couldn't look at her pretty adolescent face which was covered by too much makeup. He closed his eyes. Blackness fell over him.

"Laurence, wake up. Wake up." Her voice was far away, growing louder. "Wake up."

He awoke with Norma tapping his face and holding a pint of fresh blood. "You sure he just had alcohol in his system?"

"I didn't see him take anything else. Sorry. God, I miss Rob so badly. Sorry, sorry."

She waved his apology away. "Drink. Of course, you miss Rob. I know how much you loved him."

Laurence sucked the blood from the bag, running his fingers across the plastic to get every drop.

"You look like you stepped out of a horror movie. By the way, did you see the trailer for that movie, *Annihilation*?"

Laurence looked down, he was covered in his victim's blood. "I read the book."

"I can't wait for it. Did you see *Black Panther*?"

"No, not yet."

"You should. It was so fun to see superhero movies with all the humans on its release. I feel the audience. Did you see *Shape of Water*?"

"No, Isn't *Shape of Water* a weird ... love story." Some

sense of the world was coming back. Wasn't it rated R? "Wait, how did you see that movie? Did Derrik or Pascaline take you?"

"Carlos took me." She gestured at the driver and rubbed a wet towel on Laurence's hands, careful to clean beneath the nails. "He takes me to any movie I want. Was the book good?"

"A little strange for me, but the author, um what's his name, dang, I can almost see the cover in my head. I remember enjoying the way he described things." He closed his eyes again.

Norma pulled him upright in his seat. "You must stay awake. I saw the Andrew Wyatt Exhibit at SAM, did you go?"

"I missed it," he said.

"There's a Pre-Raphaelite exhibit in June. Maybe you'd like to go with me? You might find it inspiring."

"Why do you say that? Is the coven spying on me?"

"God, you're paranoid. I remembered you liked them: John Waterhouse, William Hunt, Danti Rosetti. Looking at your book covers, I'd say their work inspires your work now."

"You remembered?"

"Of course, I remember. Geez. You've been hooking up with my sister for years."

"It's not just a hookup. I love her."

"Yeah, I get it. I also don't care." Norma dug through the victim's wallet and pockets searching for a clue that might give a logical reason for an accidental death. There was nothing to tell them who this man had been other than a man who was willing hookup in a bar. She chewed on her bottom lip. "You paying through the app?"

"No. Cash, please. It'd look weird. I don't make big payments out of my checking account except bills."

"Even thousand. Jakub won't mind me giving you the family discount." She taped plastic over his victim. Laurence counted the cash he had on hand. $530 he had taken from his victim, and he had another $200 from other victims —

mostly homeless. "I need an ATM."

"You need a clean shirt. Finish getting that blood off you."

He shivered as he wiped off the blood. Norma handed him a fresh shirt.

Carlos stopped at an ATM in front of a credit union. He appreciated that. No fees.

Still tipsy, yet now paranoid, he wondered the best amount to withdraw. Terrified some weird amount might set off an alarm, he took out an even $300. Pocketing the extra twenty, he handed $280 to Norma.

She counted it without comment and handed him ten dollars. "Want a ride home?"

"No thanks, I'll walk. I need to clear my head."

"Well, try not to freak if you see him on the news. Don't be a stranger." Something hollow and lonely flooded Norma's voice. Knowing it was mostly the alcohol-infused blood, he was swept away by a rush of protectiveness towards the not-really-a-girl and his own grief over his lost husband. Too drunk to resist the urge to put a protective arm over Norma's slender shoulders, he whispered, "Where's Pascaline?"

"Torpor."

"What's up with this guy, Carlos? You sure he's safe?"

Her lips twisted. Her eyes twinkled with mischief. "Of course. I'm glad you couldn't tell he's a shade. We drive in the HOV lane, get into any movie I want. He even buys my victims beer on the odd days I want to get drunk."

He pulled away from her and trembled. Norma could defend herself. He had been wrong to doubt her.

"Don't look at me like that. What good does a dead body do in the ground?"

"You didn't kill him?"

"Of course not, you hypocrite! Some idiot werewolf did in a bar fight."

"You work with werewolves now too?"

She shrugged. "Seattle's an expensive city."

"Yeah. Well, be careful. If you need anything, you have my cell," he said, overcome by exhaustion and terror.

"And you have mine. Good luck finding a house."

She pulled the van's door shut behind him. As he watched the taillights disappear into traffic, he promised himself he would not lose control like that again. The city danced with drunken lights. He collapsed onto the sidewalk.

N ORMA WATCHED LAURENCE STANDING ALONE on the wet pavement, still mentally flagellating himself for his excess.

He was always rather shy, but Laurence was markedly more paranoid than normal. The bags under his eyes might be evidence he was no longer sleeping the sleep of the dead. That might be a concern. Vampires who didn't get enough sleep were known to do some crazy things.

They drove only a block when Laurence fell.

She hopped out of the back door, plucked Laurence's phone from his pocket through his phone and found his current home address. She showed Carlos who nodded but did not speak. He gathered the drunken vampire and gently set him into the seat and buckled him in. She sometimes wished shades could speak.

She sat beside Laurence and helped him drink another pint of blood, then put a cool damp cloth on his sweaty brow.

The few sentences she and Laurence shared would be the last she would share with anyone until the next vampire did something stupid. She hoped he did call her about the exhibit but figured he wouldn't.

Pascaline was the only vampire who was ever comfortable with Norma. Everybody else looked at her as evidence of their coven's shameful secret or with pity.

Older members of the Consortium wished Laurence

would come to be at home with them or at least visit with more frequency. They loved it when he and Pascaline were an item.

On paper, he was the perfect vampire: educated, artistic, good looking. No one in the coven would admit it, but they all thought he was basically the weird, boring uncle who everybody loved, but made family gatherings awkward because his interests lay outside the norm. He would nervously ramble on about the Seahawks, Mariners, Sounders, books he read, a new music style until he would trail off, say his goodnights, and leave for another decade with everyone wondering why he couldn't be a little more normal.

Even so, Agata and Jakub would question her about his well-being and remind her how much she owed Laurence, Derrik, and Pascaline for her own successes and tell her she ought to write them thank-you notes.

That's just the way they were.

Laurence probably needed more than a thank-you note.

She did a quick blood test on the victim: alcohol, molly, and Special K. What a combo. No wonder Laurence was out of it. Norma took him home, no extra charge.

As Carlos drove through the turning residential streets, Norma decided what to do with his victim's body. With all the drugs in the victim's body, she couldn't throw him to the sea monsters or offer him to the werewolves.

She drove to the Consortium. Loretta and Charles didn't leave the safety of the coterie anymore, but they still might want to party. She might make another grand before she burned him to ash.

FEBRUARY 12TH

SUNSET 5:28 PM

Chapter 8
Muddle

L AURENCE'S PHONE BUZZED NEXT TO HIS EAR. He awoke with a hangover, a rotten taste in his mouth, and a terrible feeling he didn't want to know what he had done the night before. He looked at his phone and saw a *How Was Our Service Email* from the Paper Flower Consortium and a recent text from someone named Eddie.

> Dude, what were you on last night! Carlos get you home ok? 🍻

What did I do? And who the hell are Eddie and Carlos? He was still fully dressed, but his clothes smelled like dirt, urine, and low tide.

> Yes, I'm home.

> Great! See you next week

That didn't help. He had no idea what next week was.

He logged into his bank account. Last night, he'd withdrawn $300 from an ATM. He looked through his wallet and saw he only had $20 in cash. He'd started the night with nearly $200.

He shivered. *Dear God, what did I do?*

He closed his eyes and tried to break through the fog.

Nothing.

He returned to the email and followed the link to a Survey which read: *Rate Norma's Cleaning Service, a proud subdivision of Paper Flower Consortium.*

He was still staring at his phone when another text popped up. This one from Betty.

Can I come down?

Okay. Give me 5

Crap. What did I do?

Betty never complained about his hours, but his lease did require him to be quiet during the night. He threw his dirty clothes in the hamper and redressed before he heard Betty's slow, steady tread on the outside stairs, one step at a time. He opened the door before she knocked.

"Can I make you a coffee?"

She held a tray of two glasses of water and a bottle of Ibuprofen. "How are you feeling?"

"Hung over."

"Not surprising." She handed him a glass of water and the two tablets. "Drink this before you have coffee."

"Sorry. Did I wake you when I came home?" He swallowed the two pills with the water which plummeted to his stomach. He would do better with blood, but couldn't tell Betty that.

"No. I just wanted to check on you." She smiled. "I'm having a senior moment, but I was concerned. I remember someone bringing you home, but the details are foggy."

"I woke you. Sorry."

"No, I was up. It's harder to sleep through the night now." She sighed. "Oh, my memory."

"Both our memories. I barely remember coming home, but I know from texts that Carlos drove me home."

"Carlos is a friend from one of your art meetups?"

"Yes," he said, hoping it was true.

Once Betty left, he studied his customer service survey. He could leave stars, comments or click on a box that read: *I was drunk off my ass after drinking blood from a stranger so I don't remember much, but I found myself tucked safely in my own bed, curtains drawn, fully dressed, except my shoes which I found next to the door and no mud tracked into my apartment. As I had a few texts confirming my whereabouts, my landlady was concerned about my hangover, but not overly concerned that I was a risky tenant on a bender. Norma and Carlos are the best!*

He smiled. As it seemed appropriate, he clicked the box. The app dinged and a window popped up.

He lay back on his bed and looked at his calendar. *Shit.* He had an appointment with Sarah. He considered calling her to cancel. It seemed impossible to fall in love with a house again. He wanted to hide in Betty's basement and sleep, but he needed to hunt. He needed to work. He would need a place to live.

He thought about calling Pascaline, but he didn't want to give her, or them, the wrong idea. He needed her closeness, not love. He texted Norma.

How's Pascaline?

I told you she's sleeping.

How long?

'Bout 14 years

why?

Tired.

Oh I'm missing her.

Yeah, me too. I hope she wakes soon. We've lots of movies to catch up on. She'll love Wonder Woman. If you want to hang with us you can, but no pressure.

Laurence's second alarm sounded. He rose, hurried into the shower, and threw his old clothing and his sheets into the washer. As he finished each action, he told himself to call Sarah and cancel. He did not.

The sun sank beneath the horizon. Sarah arrived, on time as always.

He opened his mouth with the urge to tell Sarah to leave, but on automatic pilot, Laurence accepted the printed listings as he clambered into the front seat.

That night, like many other nights, a drizzle fell from the sky. Due to the frequent storms, Seattle's long gray winters were legendary, sometimes extending into May. If he found a house this month, he'd seem normal to his neighbors until the long days of summer kept him inside.

He slipped his hand in his pocket and touched his ziplock bag of old earth. He wouldn't be without it again.

"There's a few properties that opened up in Wedgewood, so we'll head north and work our way south," Sarah said.

"Sounds good," he lied.

"You look beat."

"I've a commission." The second lie came more easily.

Sarah did not offer to show him houses another night, she just drove through Capitol Hill to the I-5 onramp and headed north in sluggish evening traffic until they escaped to the 85th Avenue exit.

This first house was a small two-bedroom, two-bath cottage built in 1927 with a new roof, new kitchen, and a chemical smell oozing from somewhere. It was on the bus line and close to the light rail. He wished he didn't have to cross a bridge into the city but was happy he was so far away from Georgetown. It was another definite maybe.

As Sarah had said they would, they worked their way southward. Like thieves, they slowly drove through the one-lane residential streets, stopping in front of an old fixer-upper. Then another. Then another. Nothing felt right.

Evening drew into night, Sarah's uplifting sentences became a maddening poem. "Clean freshly painted, white walls. White tile with a line of mosaic in the bathroom..."

The tiny, 700 square foot cottage was painted white to create the illusion of a larger space. As he took his first step onto the dirty carpet, his foot squished on the rotting subfloor, and he noted the slight descent into the kitchen.

"This house needs foundation work."

Laurence felt the tiny rooms close in on him and there was no place for his studio. He passed. He tried to shake his constant fear away, but every raindrop pelting the car's roof and windows reminded him: If Betty died before he found a home, he would wander until he went mad.

"THE PRICE SEEMS A LITTLE HIGH FOR SUCH a small cottage," Laurence said, looking at a little blue house which claimed to be a two bedroom with a converted basement.

"That's mostly location," Sarah said. "It has peekaboo views of Greenlake on the first floor, and from the converted attic you have a full water view. While it might not matter to you, some of the best schools are here."

He felt his hair rise on the back of his neck as soon as he stepped through the entryway. They passed the kitchen which had a new countertop, but old repainted cabinets and a strange electrical current moved through the air, putting Laurence on edge. He ran his tongue over his fangs to ensure they were not exposed. Sarah opened the door to the basement.

Rotting vegetation hit his nose.

"Hmm," Sarah said, "I guess they put the compost bin down there. Strange place for it, but with some airing, it should be fine."

She opened the door to the fenced backyard. The former owner had raised garden beds. Laurence rubbed his arms as the smell of death, not rotting, but something older entered his nostrils. This house had been the home of someone or something with whom he had no wish to do business: A hunter, a witch, maybe even another stregx. Hell, maybe a human serial killer. Whoever it was, he had to get himself and his real estate agent out of this cottage before they came home. She wouldn't understand the danger even if he explained it.

He saw the distress painted on her face as she stared into the dining room. Her heart was pounding. Maybe she *would* believe it.

"I KNOW THIS ISN'T THE ONE," LAURENCE SAID. Something had been on her mind, but Sarah wasn't seeing it until they passed the dining room's 1970's era mirrored wall. She saw the reflection of Laurence's clothing, but not of him. It was like The Invisible Man!

It might be a trick of the dim light, but she was sure it wasn't a trick.

"Sarah, I know this isn't the one. I'm ready to go."

She turned towards Laurence and noticed how large his fangs seemed. Had they grown?

"I'm sorry, but I need to take you home. I got a text from my husband. It's not an emergency, but it is serious, and I need to get home."

"Please, I'll call an Uber. You can go. No reason to drive all the way to Leschi."

While she would normally never abandon a client, Sarah was relieved. She waited for his Uber to arrive, locked up the house, and drove around for ten minutes in the rain to confirm she wasn't followed before heading home.

EVEN MORE DISHEARTENED THAN BEFORE, Laurence didn't hunt. His thirst cried, but he would need a bigger budget. Even if he wasn't a vampire, he was self-employed, he couldn't get a mortgage through a bank. He didn't want to be in debt to the Paper Flower Consortium. He had to find something under $550,000.

Chapter 9
Laurence's 3ʳᵈ Home

AFTER BILL LEFT HIM FOR THE PAPER FLOWER Consortium, Laurence realized how economically depressed the city was. He thought about leaving Seattle, but the papers claimed the Great Depression was everywhere. His old human friends died off. His victims had no cash. He couldn't sell a painting.

About to be evicted, he borrowed a year of rent from the Consortium. Bill wasn't part of the loan process, but when he discovered Laurence's plight, he visited. Dressed to the nines, his shoes sparkled, his suit was of the finest wool.

"Derrik isn't as good in bed as you are," Bill said smoothly. His icy finger stroking Laurence's cheek, he spoke of their former activities which Laurence found enjoyable. His malevolent tone debased their acts of love.

"I'll never take a dime from you," Laurence said. "I don't know what happened to you, but you've changed."

"I'm a vampire. I'm what you could be."

No longer afraid of hurting Bill, Laurence tossed him through an open window. Bill landed on his feet and walked away laughing.

Laurence found a job at an all-hours diner. It wasn't a good job, but it paid the rent. Unfortunately, he was no closer to paying off his debt. The interest's annual percentage rate was only two percent, but since he had no money to pay down the debt, the balance kept growing.

War spread throughout Europe and came to US shores. A young, healthy man was supposed to be at war. He became an oddity. He felt the whispers or longing looks. He didn't know if press gangs were still a thing, but he didn't want to find out. He developed a limp. Thankfully, only the business of war came to the Pacific Northwest, not the war itself.

Though many found work in the era of prosperity following the war, Laurence struggled to find gainful employment. He lived off humanity's scraps the way he had after Suzan died and feared going even deeper into debt.

One night, Pascaline, wearing a long black evening gown from the previous century knocked on his door. He peeked out, careful to hold it tight.

In her thick French accent, she said, "Hello, I don't know if you remember me, but I'm Pascaline. I've a proposition from Jakub."

"Please, I'll pay you. It's been hard..." He brought out his jar of pennies and nickels. "This is what I collected. Few have money. They have Green Stamps and bonds, but cash is still rare unless I kill only the wealthy. Give him this, let him know I'm trying..."

She smiled wanly. "God above, you're as paranoid as Agata warned us you'd be. Jakub has a job for you to pay off your debt."

"A job?"

"It is nothing the coven believes you would find distasteful. May I come in?"

Laurence let her inside and invited her to sit.

"William created a vampire from an uneducated farm girl of just fourteen."

"William ... you mean Bill? My Bill?"

"Yes. He thought he could control a child," Pascaline said, "practice his 'brainwashing techniques' before establishing his own coven. He said as much before we killed him."

"Bill is dead?"

"I'm sorry you feel loss, but my concern is for Norma."

"No, he wouldn't do that. Bill wasn't a monster." Laurence was overcome by sorrow, but he had wept too many bloody tears over Bill already. His knees buckled. "You blame me?"

"Why would we blame you?" Pascaline met his eyes. "He went through the program. None of us foresaw the problem. William was charming."

"You think I would harm a child? That I'm a monster too?"

Pascaline's scarlet mouth became an O. "No, you misunderstand. Agata already adopted her into the coven. Derrik and I are tasked to teach her to be a vampire. What we ask of you is to teach her arithmetic and home economics. If she has questions that we can't answer, perhaps you might."

"What do you mean 'questions?'"

"You live in the modern world. Like Norma, no one sang songs as you were reborn or held your hands during your first days. She was alone when she died. He kept her locked in a barn."

"Pascaline, please," Laurence interrupted her. "I know Bill. He wouldn't have hurt a child."

"Your loyalty to William is admirable, but the fact is he took a lonely, studious girl. He sliced open her ankle and drained her to the point of death. Then forced her to drink his blood from a cup."

"Her ankle?"

"He told her he was Achilles reborn. He tried to control her with myths and stories. When that didn't work, he simply punished her. He kept her confused and frightened.

"Now, Agata must hold her to get her to sleep in a coffin. It's a struggle to get her to bathe. She fought Loretta off when she tried to dress her in proper clothing."

Laurence cringed at her words. He didn't know what to say about Bill, the barn, the coffin. The dress seemed the safest bet. "You mean a dress like yours?"

"Well, yes."

He slowly walked around her, looking at the buttons and lacing, not to mention the bustle and ruffles. "I don't think a young girl would know how to put it on."

"What should she know?"

Laurence almost laughed, but Pascaline was earnest. And her scarlet lips were irresistible.

He dug through his end table until he found a magazine. He found an ad with a family riding bikes to a picnic. The daughter wore pedal pushers and a matching sweater and blouse, but Pascaline's eyes were on the mother who wore a plaid dress.

"I can't believe women go around showing their legs like that," she said. "How is everyone so hairless? Even the father."

"They aren't. The painter just didn't paint the body hair. Many women shave or wax. I suppose it's been a while since you left the coven?"

"I don't leave often, no. The world is much brighter than it was. Sometimes, I'm afraid I won't know the dawn."

God, she looked so soft, he wanted to touch her creamy skin. He ignored the urge. "I fear that too." Laurence found in spite of himself: he was in love again — or at least a healthy lust.

"You buy your clothes in stores?"

"Yes."

"You know how to shop in them?" Pascaline removed a thin cotton floral blouse from her bag. By its tag, it originally came from Sears and said Girls Size 12. "Even if you won't tutor her, will you show me this new world? I have her measurements and her shirt, but clothing stores don't make sense to me. I mean, really, what does a 12 even mean? And worse, the 12 is different in all the stores and the sales clerks won't come near me. I don't understand catalogs very well, I'm afraid. There are so many new fabrics."

Laurence stared at the shirt. It looked small in her delicate gloved hands. "So, Jakub will discharge my debt if I teach Norma arithmetic and home economics? But you have an accountant and secretaries."

She frowned. "As far as we know, you're the only

vampire in Seattle who was born lost. Besides, what else do you have to do that's so pressing?"

"But Bill..."

"Is dead. Norma is undead and needs us to guide her."

Pascaline was so beautiful. He ached to be of service to her and those red lips. "I can accompany you to a department store, where would you like to go: Sears, Nordstrom's, Bon Marche?"

"What would give us the best quality?"

DURING NORMA'S FIRST FOUR YEARS AS A strega, Laurence and Pascaline had a love affair. He adored her unchanging beauty and the calm demeanor of someone who had lived for three centuries.

He grew to understand the coven better, but he could not trust them. Even with undead evidence of Bill's crime, Laurence simply couldn't believe someone he had once loved was capable of monstrosity. Norma's rebirth was simply an accident as his had been.

Norma was never a problem, at least not for Laurence. She did her assignments on time; she took the quizzes. Pascaline or Derrik would sit nearby and read. In the rare moments she felt overwhelmed, they would sit beside her and stroke her hair until those moments passed. They promised her if she would only sleep during the day like a normal vampire, she'd be awake for her lessons, but no one would hurt her, no one was angry. They had all the time in the world.

Laurence's old dreams of having a family preoccupied him, but he couldn't give Pascaline a better life than the one she had. Norma had an entire coven who adored her. All he could do is tutor Norma in arithmetic and home accounting, which, at the girl's request, became business accounting, philosophy, and ethics.

Though the other vampires did not change, Pascaline dressed in modern clothing to match Norma as she had seen in magazines or store windows.

To reward her good behavior, Pascaline often took Norma to late-night films with Laurence and Derrik as their escorts. Poor Derrik, born and reborn in the Victorian era, was shocked to see what humans considered family entertainment. Pascaline found this amusing considering that European families of every class used to watch executions when she was a girl. Laurence had to agree with Pascaline.

Norma loved the illusion of movies and the puzzle of taking apart the illusion. She often explained the camera tricks and optical effects they had seen, so Derrik didn't worry so much. He still worried.

While Norma couldn't finish maturing outwardly, she did mentally. She left tutors behind and begged Agata for night classes at the University of Washington.

Once the three didn't have Norma's care, Derrik's presence faded back into the coven. All Laurence and Pascaline didn't have in common came into focus. He slept in a bed; she slept in a coffin. He hunted each night; she drank from animals or a willing victim whom she did not kill. Though she organized several charity drives throughout the year to help the homeless or the environment, like many well-bred ladies of her era, she never held a job in the traditional sense.

The night their formal relationship ended, Pascaline thought to enjoy a film, but he argued about the costs of tickets. "I invited you," she said, meaning she, as always, planned to pay.

"Yes, you're a woman of leisure," he said snidely.

"Well, what would you like to see?"

He argued about how they should be doing more important things than going to movies. He didn't even know why. He had no interest in helping those less fortunate; he ate them.

He did not notice the single drop of blood rolled

down her cheek, only the stain left behind. "Good evening, Laurence." She handed him a jar of old dirt from the Coven cellar and left his apartment. He followed and begged her not to leave him as she scooped dirt from a planting bed in his apartment complex into another jar.

"You know where I am," she said softly. "What I am."

He agonized for months after she left, he picked up the phone a thousand times, but couldn't speak to the operator and ask her to dial the number.

Still, every few years, Pascaline would grace his doorstep. She asked if he would like to share an evening together. He never said no.

Those evenings would sometimes linger into weeks until they drifted apart. Laurence and Pascaline shared no hopes or dreams, just the loneliness of immortality, trust, and sexual compatibility.

She only stopped coming after he met Rob.

FEBRUARY 15TH

SUNSET 5:32

Chapter 10
A new listing

OUT OF HABIT, LAURENCE SCANNED NEW listings. He found a little house in Madison Valley. He emailed Sarah the MLS number and waited for her reply. By the time he had gone to bed, she still hadn't answered.

Of course, she's probably asleep, he told himself. Except he remembered her face. She had been terrified.

He forced himself to lie down. He couldn't sleep.

At noon, he opened his phone. Still no reply. He drifted off for a while. 4 pm. No reply.

He kept thinking about her expression. *Oh God, had she seen my fangs? Did I sweat blood?* She must have seen something. *Damn me. Do I need a new Realtor?*

He liked Sarah and didn't want to start over. By the houses she was showing him, she was closing in on the perfect one.

He texted Norma.

> Hey if I scared my Realtor, what should I do?

> I'll take care of everything for $300

> You won't hurt anyone, will you?

His phone rang.

"Don't be stupid. I'm gonna make your agent trust you. Tell me everything that happened," Norma said.

Laurence described the strange feeling he had in that house and Sarah's face.

"Was she looking at you?"

"No, the dining room."

"What's the address?"

"I don't want you going there!"

"Address?" Norma repeated.

"What if you're hurt?"

"Address. I won't ask a third time."

He gave it to her.

"Email your Realtor. Tell her your little sister is in town for midwinter break and ask if it's okay if I tag along when you go look at houses."

"How's that going to help if she saw my fangs?"

"Just tell her." Norma sighed. "And to counter any doubt, we'll view houses in the day if we need to."

"The day?" Laurence's stomach dropped.

"I'll smother us in sunscreen. We'll be fine."

"What about the parts you can't cover with sunscreen?"

"UV sunglasses, brimmed hat, earmuffs. It's February. It's going to be overcast."

"I've a favor. Can I pay after I close?"

"Yes. Or we could do installments if your house search goes long. Don't worry. We won't do anything that'll look weird to *them*."

"Great, thanks."

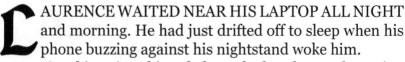

LAURENCE WAITED NEAR HIS LAPTOP ALL NIGHT and morning. He had just drifted off to sleep when his phone buzzing against his nightstand woke him.

Sarah's voice chirped through the phone, shattering

his grogginess. "A few new listings just came on the market I think you'll want to see. I know you normally don't go out in the day, but it's supposed to rain pretty hard tomorrow."

"You don't think we can see them at night?"

"I don't know if I can go out again at night for a few weeks." Sarah's voice took on the edge of fear. Laurence could almost hear her heart beat over the phone.

"Oh ... and you're okay if I bring my sister to look at houses? She's a teenager so she won't break anything or run around. It's just she's here."

"Of course, she's welcome." Sarah's voice became more natural. She'd pick them up tomorrow at eleven am.

Chapter 11
Laurence's 4th Home

RELIEVED SARAH TRUSTED HIM AGAIN, Laurence continued to build up color on his canvas. Using the fat over lean method as he was taught centuries before, he refined his shadows. With thicker layers of paint, he softened some lines and tightened others.

When he finished painting for the night, he touched the jars holding the dirt from Rob's house. He couldn't bring himself to unscrew the lid. It didn't matter, he could easily remember previous decades.

During the 60's and 70's, Pascaline visited Laurence when she wished. She remained mostly in the coven, while he moved about in downtown efficiency apartments to hide his lack of aging. He kept a low profile during the changing political landscape but watched with excitement as humans marched for civil rights. He observed the moon landing and believed the Age of Aquarius was just around the corner.

The 80's happened instead.

He worked as an evening courier for several law offices. The pay was good, and Seattle was still a small enough city, he remained mostly unnoticed. In 1990, he met Robert Garcia when he delivered notarized files the law office's client's accounting firm.

As a CPA, Rob dressed for work, wore his dark hair short, and had a way of putting people at ease. He thanked Laurence for the file and shook his hand.

All Laurence thought about Robert Garcia C.P.A. constantly and hoped work would cause their paths to cross again. It didn't.

He waited at Rob's office and followed him to a bar. He

tapped him on the shoulder. Over the loud rock music which would soon be known as Grunge, he half-shouted, "Hi, aren't you Robert? We met at your office last week."

Rob's eyes squinted a bit. "Laurence, right?"

He remembered my name!

They moved towards a window where the music wasn't so loud and spoke for a little while. Rob knew himself, knew his calling, and had put up with way too much shit when he was younger both for being gay and for being not what everyone wanted in a Latin lover to give a shit about what people thought of him now. He loved being an accountant. He loved helping people.

Totally smitten, Laurence told him he had a secret. "I understand if you don't want to be with me. I — I..."

"Spit it out. What is it, HIV?"

"I'm a stregone."

"What's that? A disability?" Rob said, his eyes raised.

He hated it, but he knew only one way to describe it. "Like a vampire."

"Metaphorically?"

"No. Really." He showed him his fangs.

"I got to go." Rob stood and threw money on their table.

"Wait." Laurence grabbed his wrist. "Please call me." Laurence shoved his card into his hand. Rob hurried out of the bar without glancing behind him.

Laurence shuffled home, assuming he would never see Rob again.

However, two nights later, Rob's soft voice echoed through his phone. "Laurence, do you believe you're a vampire?"

"Yes."

"You need some help, man."

"Probably."

"Do you want to drink my blood?"

"No! I just want to know you. I liked your smile that

day that we met at your office. When I saw you again, I just knew I wanted to talk to you. God, I sound like an idiot. I like you."

Rob quietly rattled off the name of a 24-hour café where he was willing to meet IF Laurence would swear on the cross that he wasn't planning on drinking his blood. "Or can you do that?"

"Swear on the cross, sure. I'm Catholic, if it matters..."

"You go to church?"

"Only on Christmas. I ought to go more often. Do you attend church?"

"I take my grandmother every Sunday. She can't drive. But she's the only family member who'll talk to me now. Damn, what in hell am I doing? Why can't I get you out of my head?"

"I don't know, but I hope you'll meet me," Laurence said.

They met at the café.

Rob ordered a waffle; Laurence ordered a bloody steak. While they waited for their food, Rob placed a beautiful tiger's eye rosary on the table.

"Swear on it."

Laurence took it in his hand. "I swear I've no designs on drinking your blood or turning you into a vampire. Though I prefer if you called me a stregone."

"You didn't burn."

"Only the sun can harm me, that's why I work as an evening courier." He handed it back to Rob.

"So you aren't damned?"

"No. I was attacked and sexually assaulted. I fought her off."

"So..."

"Honestly, it's an STD. It made me allergic to sunlight. I don't know if I'll live forever or just a long time.

"I've never made another. I always use condoms. I need blood, but I'm not a sadist or into any rough stuff. In my long years, I was married once, but she died. I had a boyfriend for fifteen years, but that ended badly. I had a girlfriend for four years which ended because we didn't have much in common. We're still friends though. So, that's it. I won't hurt you. I like you."

They talked for a while and made a date for the next night.

L AURENCE TRIED TO SCRAPE THE DRIED OIL paint off his tiles in his kitchenette. He wanted his apartment to be spotless before Rob arrived. It was small, but it looked pretty good. His sheets were freshly laundered though he tried not to feel too optimistic about that night's activities. He beheld the unframed canvases lining his walls. He hoped it wasn't too gauche to hang one's own paintings. He vacuumed the carpet, ran the Hoover over his couch and threw the throw pillows in the dryer to fluff them. He dressed in his only button-down shirt and hoped it looked nice enough.

Rob was as handsome as he was the other night. Laurence noticed he still wore his crucifix — even though Laurence already proved it didn't affect him.

"Can I get you some wine?" Laurence asked.

"Sure."

"So, these are yours?"

Laurence hurried to pour the wine. His own was mixed with blood. Rob's was the best wine Laurence could afford.

He handed him his glass.

"Wow. I can't believe you painted these. Why are you a courier?"

"Well, I painted full-time once, but then when the economy turned south, I needed to go back to work."

"There's lots of art shows in the area."

Laurence bit his lip. "I don't know..."

"What's stopping you?"

"My old boyfriend didn't like my painting. He called me a pretender."

"Where is this boyfriend?" Rob said.

"He dumped me. He hated me near the end because I wouldn't turn him into a stregone. He ... well ... like I said, it ended badly."

"Forget him," Rob said.

"I can't forget him. We were together for fifteen years, and he left me for another stregone."

"Then remember the good parts of the relationship and turn off his negative voice in your head. You can be a painter if that's what you want."

Laurence didn't know what he wanted other than to be with Rob and worthy of his goodness.

Five months later, Laurence moved into Rob's lovely little bungalow on First Hill.

THE YEARS WENT BY QUICKLY. HOW INTENSELY they kissed when they kissed. How Rob cared for him. How Rob encouraged him. Rob didn't need anything from him except mutual love.

For the first time in his long years, Laurence decided to be an artist, not a pretender. As a full-time painter, he kept business hours, called galleries and even participated in the nighttime art walk. He made prints and greeting cards out of his more popular pieces.

Rob's dark hair grayed around his temples, and he developed crow's-feet around the eyes, but he had true vigor in his step. Laurence wove a few strands of gray into his own hair to look older but otherwise remained the same.

Undead life was perfect until 2005. Laurence grew

edgy and irritable. He found he couldn't sleep after dawn. He cried over everything: weddings in movies, breakups in movies, pictures of families. A dead rat who had been hit by a car made him hysterical.

"Why don't you go to the doctor?" Rob asked. "Aren't there stregoni doctors?"

Laurence feared telling Rob about the coven, so he did not. "No. There are legends of stregx sometimes needing to go into a deep sleep for a few years. It might be my time, but I don't want to leave you. I've never loved anyone like I love you."

Rob embraced him. "I love you. But if you need sleep — even ten years of sleep — then you do. Everything will be fine. The house is in my name, there's plenty of money. I'm in good health. I'll just be a little more wrinkled that's all. Who knows maybe when you wake up, these messed-up laws will have changed, and we can actually get married."

Laurence agreed. He would love to be married again.

They researched the problem together, though Laurence was careful to never mention the Paper Flower Consortium. Rob and Laurence moved a bed into the basement with his jars of earth. Rob tucked him under two warm quilts and kissed his lips then kissed his brow. "Everything will be fine. You just need sleep."

Rob walked each day to his accounting office, ate a low carb diet and remained somewhat trim. They had a solid savings and investment plan. Rob shouldn't have died so young!

Laurence didn't know if he ever would be able to marry again, but if someday someone wanted to bond themselves to him, he swore he would be a better companion and remember they were mortal. And he would keep the house in his name.

FEBRUARY 17
SUNSET 5:36 PM

Chapter 12
A New Day

NORMA KNOCKED ON LAURENCE'S DOOR AS THE light edged towards the horizon. He ushered her inside and slammed it shut against the coming inferno.

"What's wrong with you?" she asked.

"It's so close to dawn." Laurence peeked through his window. He didn't want to go out there. He spent nearly two centuries safe, waiting for the sunset.

"You've got to calm down, or this won't work. Did you feed?"

"Yes."

"Look at me."

She could have passed as a human teenager. She dressed in warm layers of fleece and Gortex as every Seattlite did in February. She smiled.

"Your fangs are missing! How'd you do that?"

"Ever seen that show *Faceoff*?" She removed her jacket, pullover, cap, and scarf. She held it out for a moment, then tossed them on a nearby chair.

"Uh, no." He realized he should have offered to take it, but Norma was moving too fast.

"Any allergies to latex or silicone?" She opened her purple backpack emblazoned with happy kittens and pulled out a tackle box.

"How would I know?"

"Ever had a reaction to gloves, condoms, that sort of thing?"

"No. Can our kind have a reaction?" Laurence asked.

"I've only tested this on Derrik and myself, so I don't know," Norma said. "How much time do we have?"

"Sarah will pick us up at eleven," Laurence said.

"Great, plenty of time to do a test. I can paint the tips of your fangs away, but it's not as natural looking. You must remain calm and without bloodlust, because the silicone will stretch some, but if your fangs suddenly expand, it can tear."

"I have no bloodlust for Sarah," Laurence said. "Where's Carlos?"

"Bingeing on Netflix."

"It's safe to leave him alone?"

"He has lots of snacks."

"He doesn't eat brains?"

"No. Raw broccoli. He's on this whole foods/paleo thing," Norma said. "I brought some bronzers to add color to your cheeks."

"But…"

"It's only SPF 25, but that will be on top of this face cream."

"I don't want to look like a clown."

"I'm going to dust your cheeks and temples with a few layers of color as if the wind is biting — which it is. You'll look a little pinker. That's it. Also, it will guarantee you cast a reflection," Norma said.

"A reflection?"

"Yeah. I checked at that house. The dining room wall was mirrored."

He lowered his voice though he didn't know why. "What do you think was there?"

"I think an ancient witch. Whoever it was, I didn't want to mess with her. I got out of there fast."

FROM HER CAR, SARAH SAW LAURENCE USHER his little sister across the yard, careful she stayed under the umbrella though it was barely raining. He opened the door to the back seat and ensured Norma was safely inside before he got into the front. His head was down and covered with his hat and hoodie.

His cheeks were redder than before.

"You're okay. We were only outside for a second." The girl put out her fleeced gloved hand to Sarah. "Hi, I'm Norma."

"I'm Sarah. Nice to meet you."

The girl's fingers were icy, but her palm was warm enough. She had dark curls every woman would die for and a pretty ivory complexion like her brother. Most importantly, she didn't have fangs.

Sarah adjusted her mirrors. She could see Laurence's reflection! *It must have just been a trick of the light. It was night. He has dark hair and those hoodies cast shadows all over his face.*

Norma took a selfie over her brother's shoulder which obviously put Laurence in the shot.

"We didn't burn," he said.

"It's cloudy," Norma said. She leaned back and buckled her seatbelt. "You worry too much."

Sarah handed Laurence the printed listings. He thanked her in his quiet way.

She observed Laurence had removed his fangs. *It must be a kink if he's keeping it from his sister.*

Norma's eyes were on her phone as her thumbs flew over the touchscreen.

"What do you like to use? Snapchat?" Sarah asked, thinking of her own daughters' near constant use.

"Yep." She leaned forward to show Sarah the image. The selfie of her and Laurence had a sparkling filter on it, and she had put silly hunting hats on them. The caption read: *On the hunt for my brother's new house.*

Already a few friends liked it. Laurence did not seem amused.

Though Laurence didn't seem to enjoy chatting,

Norma had no problem filling the car with noise. She spoke of how their mom kept track of her on Snapchat, but she still had to call every night since "Seattle and all."

Norma had taken the ferry and bus several times to Laurence's before, or to their other brother's house, but this time she was allowed to travel alone which made it easier since her brothers kept the worst schedule due to their disability. So far, Laurence had taken her to SAM and 5th Avenue Theatre. On Saturday, they were going to a theater in Capitol Hill, which sometimes had good shows. She loved that her brothers lived in Seattle so she could go to the theater often. He was busy working on a new painting. Her other brother was a lawyer.

Laurence gave his younger sister an unreadable look over his shoulder. Sarah guessed since Laurence kept his own chatter at personal affairs to a minimum, he might be annoyed.

Norma didn't even seem to notice. "Do you like going to the theater?"

"Occasionally. It's a once-a-year event for my family — often a show at Christmastime."

Norma asked if Sarah ever went to the ACT's rendition of the Christmas Carol which she thought was very good.

Sarah agreed ACT put on a wonderful show.

L AURENCE COULDN'T BELIEVE THE NON-STOP blather coming from Norma's lips and the sudden display of teenaged behavior. Norma slipped into humanity so naturally, it scared him. She was 120 years younger than he, but she mimicked humans so much better, and her intelligence was almost alien. She knew how to ensure she cast a reflection and how to take pictures of herself. Pascaline didn't know these things. Derrik didn't know these things. *What else did she know?*

As they walked into the first house, Norma posed for another selfie.

"Some people don't like their addresses shown," Sarah said.

"I won't get the numbers," Norma promised. "Want in?"

Sarah slipped into the frame in a natural way. Norma clicked and showed Sarah the picture. *How did Sarah know how to do a selfie? Or more importantly, why don't I?*

Sarah approved of the picture before they toured the house.

Laurence studied the small living room as Norma looked at her phone. The gas fireplace was a nice feature but had a flat 1980's surround in flat black with gold splatters in it. Several stains discolored the old carpeting, but the walls looked clean and in good repair.

He jumped when Norma asked, "What's the Internet like in this neighborhood?"

"I'm not sure," Sarah said.

"Did Laurence tell you he has a home office? He needs high-speed Internet," Norma insisted.

"I can find out," Sarah said. "Cable and DSL are in 98 percent of neighborhoods; fiber is much less common."

Norma nodded and leaned on a wall near the door, playing with her phone.

Sarah led Laurence through the house. "I'm sorry," he said softly to her back. He gestured at Norma.

Sarah smiled. "She's fine. All kids have their noses in their phones."

"I meant her tone. I'll speak to her."

"Laurence, really, she's fine. Internet speeds are a fair question. Besides, don't you remember when you knew everything?"

"Yes. I guess so." Not knowing what else to say, Laurence felt the draft from the windows.

"The kitchen's nice, but the stove is electric, and the listing mentions a gas connection," Norma said suddenly. "Is the gas just for the fireplace in the living room?"

"Might be," Sarah said. "Want to check the basement? We can see what the gas lines are for."

Norma agreed. Laurence wondered if she was shopping for herself or for him.

THEY CIRCLED SEATTLE'S SOUTHERN neighborhoods, searching for the perfect home among the fixer-uppers and foreclosed derelicts in his budget. It had been uncomfortable with just Sarah, but it was unbearable with Norma in the back seat watching him, watching Sarah, pretending to play with her phone, pretending to be a human girl making meaningless conversation.

The light of the day streaming into their windows was diffused only by cloud cover. It was stupid going out in the day. He put his hand in his pocket and felt his Ziplock bag of earth.

HEADING UP THE MAIN ARTERIAL TO BEACON Hill, he loathed the neighborhood where he lost the other house. They passed the grocery store and bakery and turned to the side streets. The same view which he hadn't gotten mocked him.

"This rambler came on the market yesterday. It's another fixer-upper. The only thing is it has a crawlspace, no basement. Two bedrooms, one and a half bath. No garage, but it does have a paved driveway," Sarah said brightly.

The rain lightened to a drizzle by the time they got

up the hill. Sarah parked her car in the driveway. The wood siding had been painted purple and pink.

"That's so cute," Norma said.

"Uh, I don't know if cute is the word I'd use," Laurence said. "Remember, that's just paint," Sarah said as if she knew what Laurence was thinking. Maybe she did. The color scheme was hideous.

The rain stopped. Sunlight burst from the clouds. Laurence glanced at Norma. She did not seem unnerved, but she waited for him to open the umbrella.

His unease grew with each step to the front walk. The sun spilled on the umbrella. He couldn't stop himself from checking his baseball cap and hoodie, then he drew Norma's hood over her ski-cap.

"We'll be fine, just stay under the umbrella," she whispered. He pulled Norma closer to his chest: both to protect her and use her as a shield.

Sarah fiddled with the lock and loose doorknob. She pushed on it with her shoulder.

What was taking so long? Laurence felt his fangs expand. He no longer cared about finding a home, he only wished to escape the sun.

"Don't." Norma pinched his hand sharply with her fingernails.

His fangs retracted.

Norma glanced into his face. He opened his mouth. "Good. Silicone intact," she whispered.

"There we go." Sarah smiled as she got the door open.

They stepped inside. He was careful to only close the umbrella once he was sure the sun could not reach them.

The living room had two small windows of the mid-century era over a river rock fireplace. The east facing window was larger but still a standard size. His heart opened as he never believed it might open again. "Can you imagine if those little windows were replaced with stained glass?" He found himself asking aloud.

Sarah nodded. "What pattern do you like?"

"Mission style would go with the mid-century vibe of this place."

"Oh my God, I love the dining room." Norma peeked through the French doors into the dining room. "You know, this would make a good art studio and its close to the kitchen for coffee and to wash your brushes."

"I suppose it would." He tried not to get too excited.

He moved through the dining room and into the kitchen. He turned on the faucet; it worked. "Everything looks well-kept."

Norma pointed out the window. It was still sunny and getting warmer. Another door led to the back which held a covered patio overlooking a nice-sized yard. Norma took the umbrella and stepped outside.

She came back in. "Pretty quiet. Looks like there might be a bit of drainage issue near the fence. It puddles."

Norma opened a cupboard door and measured the inside with an App on her phone, then she texted the measurements to Laurence. "It's a little sticky, but I think that's a pretty good-sized kitchen."

"Solid wood. They'd be nice refinished," Laurence said.

"This home has only had two owners. The current owners are retiring and looking to downsize to a condo," Sarah said.

A hallway led to the two bedrooms and bathroom. A bit of cat urine stained the old carpeting in the smaller of the two bedrooms, but that could be replaced with minimal investment.

"Norma, would you measure these rooms?" he asked. "Think my bedroom furniture would fit?"

He pretended to study both rooms again as Norma quickly took the measurements, careful not to step in the sunbeam pouring through the window in the southern-facing room.

"What are you thinking?" Sarah asked.

That the sun will kill me.

"I'm thinking maybe I'd take the smaller room to sleep in and put a library and guest room in the bigger room. Studio in the dining room. The living room will be my TV room. Where was the washer and dryer hookups?"

"I saw them in here." Norma opened the door which he had thought was a closet.

"Do those stay?"

"The listing says all appliances," Sarah said.

"The light rail station is near the Red Apple a few blocks away, right?" he asked, though they passed them on the way in.

"Yes."

Outside, the sun still spilled between clouds.

"There's an attic up there?" Norma said.

"Looks like it." Sarah pulled on the rope which brought down the stairs.

He climbed them, peeked around and only saw insulation, venting systems, and minimal rodent droppings. He climbed down.

Clouds covered the horizon again.

He walked into the bathroom and pretended to study the plumbing under the sink until drizzle hit the windows.

"This is the one." He read the listing again. "I want to put in a full price, $529,000 cash offer dependent upon inspection right away. Today, if you can."

Sarah smiled. "I can write up the paperwork today, but don't get your hopes up for a reply until tomorrow. Maybe the day after. And there might be more than one offer. It'd be good if you wrote a letter to the homeowner."

"Does that really work? I thought that was just an HGTV thing."

"In this case, you ought to tell them you're not an investor. This house gives me the vibe the owner wants a family to live here."

"ARE WE GOING TO GET INTO A BIDDING WAR?" Laurence asked Norma as she wiped the makeup off his face.

"Don't be silly."

"Would Derrik..."

"Don't move." She carefully peeled the silicone from his gums. "Be mad I mentioned a brother? Probably not. But I also don't see why he is going to know. You going to tell him?"

"No, but what if Sarah asks for a referral?"

"Look, now she trusts you. She believes you have a weird kink, but you're not a dangerous weirdo."

After trying to rub the tingling away, he spat into a napkin. "Some dangerous weirdos have little sisters."

"I suppose some do," she said removing her own makeup. "But Sarah thinks you're only a part-time weirdo. You found another house today. Hopefully, they'll accept your offer. You'll get through the inspections, and everything will be perfect."

FEBRUARY 19
SUNSET 5:38

Chapter 13
Acceptance

LAURENCE DID NOT GO TO SLEEP FOR THE REST of the day. He paced his basement apartment even as his eyes grew heavy, even as the thirst overwhelmed his senses. As night came again, he needed to feed, but he was too on edge to feel peace.

Midnight. He needed to leave now if he were to have time to hunt. He went to SoDo, hoping to bump into Norma and thank her. He wandered the streets until he found a dive. He found a man who complained about some woman whom he loved and hated with seemingly equal measure.

After listening to this man's never-ending rant, it was a pleasure to drink his blood and bury him in the transfer center's compost bin.

He arrived home one hour before sunrise. He removed his dirty and stained clothing and started a load of laundry.

Once his clothes were in the dryer, he lay on his bed wanting to sleep, but sleep would not come. When the dryer binged, he rose and folded his clothes. He tried to sleep again, but he couldn't. Every minute in bed, he wondered if this time he got the house or if an investor would swoop in and steal it. He tried to paint, but nothing felt right as sunrise became morning and then afternoon.

He leapt to his feet as his cell phone vibrated. Sarah Martin's name was on the screen.

"You got the house, congratulations," she said.

"Thank you so much! I'm so happy!"

They spoke of the next steps which Laurence was to do.

He wanted to call someone, but Pascaline was in

torpor. He wasn't part of The Paper Flower Consortium. He put his phone on the charger.

He sat at his easel and painted the redheaded woman; by midnight, he'd finished it, and he was ready to hunt. His painting was sublime, but it wasn't the woman from the bar. It somehow morphed into a more human version of Pascaline.

FEBRUARY 22
SUNSET 5:44 PM

Chapter 14
Inspection

THOUGH NORMA SHOWED LAURENCE HOW TO remain "uncindered" when the sun was up, he was careful to stay out of its lethal beams as much as possible. His eyes kept closing as he walked through the house with the inspector, Mike Patrick, and Sarah beside him.

Mike discovered some minor mold, a few missing shingles from the roof which would need to be replaced, and antiquated, below-code plumbing. He also found dried mouse poop and a mouse mummy in the attic. The electrical could be upgraded, but it wasn't as necessary as the plumbing and roof.

Overall, the surprises didn't change anything. The location was perfect, and the home's layout was perfect for Laurence. After a quiet discussion, it was decided they would ask for a drop in price of $5,000 to pay to upgrade the below-code plumbing.

"Are you sure?" He asked. "I really want the house."

"It'll be fine," Sarah said.

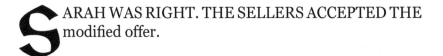

SARAH WAS RIGHT. THE SELLERS ACCEPTED THE modified offer.

MARCH 21ST
SUNSET 7:24

Chapter 15
Final Inspection

THE DAY BEFORE CLOSING, LAURENCE rechecked the file box he had set aside for all the paperwork he received throughout the process: contract, proof of title search, appraisal, inspection reports, and closing disclosures. He had already requested the cashier's check from Monte dei Paschi di Siena.

He checked the weather report and crossed his fingers. Cloudy!

He put on a bit of the bronzer he acquired from Norma to make certain he looked even more human. He added sunscreen, a Mariner's cap, sunglasses, gloves. Then he put a Mariner's hoodie over it all.

The sun broke through the clouds. He scooted closer to the other side of the back seat of his Uber. Even the filtered sun caused his skin to prickle. Blood-tinged sweat dripped from Laurence's forehead. He desired relief no matter what form. His fangs expanded as he looked at the back of the Uber driver's head. He imagined the sweetness of ripping open the man's throat.

That would definitely bring down my Uber rating.

He gently massaged his temples and took a deep breath, followed by another. *I will ignore the pain.* Every moment in the sun, it became harder to disregard the sensation of burning, to swallow the pain, and the inner voice telling him to go home to Betty's basement where the sun couldn't touch him.

"You okay?" the driver asked.

"Migraine."

"Oh, the wife gets those; totally sucks. Sorry, man."

The car stopped.

He said, "Have a good day" to the driver, hurried toward the house, and knocked on the door.

He was terrified that, with his undeadness showing, he'd spoil the deal, but he had to escape the sun.

Karen Harris opened the door. She appeared to be in her sixties.

"Why, you must be Laurence, come in."

"Thank you, Ms. Harris." He forced himself to enter calmly as the sun's heat radiated across his shoulders.

"Please call me Karen."

He shook the lady's hand. Her pulse reminded him of Betty. He focused on acting like a human. "Thank you, Karen. I'm very excited for tomorrow. I hope I'm not intruding too much on your time."

Careful to stay away from the windows, he removed his hat and sunglasses, shoved them into the hoodie's large pocket.

"You look very flushed, would you like a bottle of water?"

Laurence didn't, but he accepted the water bottle. "Thanks. That's so kind of you."

Karen finished dumping the contents of the fridge into the garbage. "I hoped I'd be all done before you got here, but it looks like we'll need to make another dump run. Everything seems to take longer than I think it will and I found some stuff my kids may or may not want in the attic."

By her tempo, Laurence realized she didn't want to cloud the deal either! She wanted to sell the house and move on to the next chapter of her life.

"Yes, I understand that. I'll try to do my inspection quickly and get out of your way."

"Well, I'm about finished here; please let me know when you leave."

Laurence didn't see any new issues with the house. The faucets still worked. The drains still drained. Karen had obviously been consistent about her method of cleaning. Each room was emptied, the closet doors left open and post-it note checklists on the door that said "Empty, Window sills, Vacuum." Both bathroom cupboards were wide open as were all the built-ins. As promised, Karen had emptied the property and left everything in good condition. He went back into the kitchen and happy to see she packed the garbage into her car. He thanked her for her time and called another Uber.

Unless the world ended tonight, he would have a home!

MARCH 22ND

SUNSET 7:26

Chapter 16
In closing

THE WORLD DID NOT END.

Laurence walked towards his Uber. *God, I can't wait to be a creature of the night again. How does Norma stay up so late on a semi-regular basis?*

He rubbed his tongue against his fangs to confirm they were not forward, but his skin tingled. He should have put on another layer of sunscreen. He didn't know how much more daytime living he could take.

"Wait a second!" Betty popped out of the front door. She wobbled a little as she stepped downstairs clenching the handrail.

Laurence shortened the distance between them.

"Watch that blood sugar now," she said. "You take this and if you get the shakes..." She pressed a bottle containing a bright red liquid into his hands. It looked like Kool-Aid.

"Uh."

"I won't hear another word about it. You take it now."

LAURENCE WAS HAPPY THAT THE ESCROW office didn't have outside windows so he could sit where the sun didn't hit him at closing, but he was nervous to be in the room with the handsome human named Scott. At least in Washington State, he didn't have to meet the sellers again at closing and worry about scaring them out of the deal; just Scott: whose rich brown flesh looked and smelled beautiful.

He is not prey, Laurence reminded himself.

Laurence handed Scott his passport, hoping that the Paper Flower Consortium's work would withstand scrutiny.

The escrow agent made a copy and attached it to his file without comment.

He handed him the receipt for the wire transfer.

"Monte dei Paschi di Siena, that's not one I see every day," he said.

"I've family still in Italy."

"Ah-h, Italy is such a beautiful country; I hope to visit someday," Scott said as he scanned the information. "What part?"

"Venice."

"How nice," he said in a conversational tone, but the words also hinted that he didn't really care. Laurence was just another appointment he had to get through. He turned the first page in the pile of documents and had Laurence sign.

Laurence trembled as his fangs expanded, mesmerized by Scott's pulse. The man turned each page over, described it, and pointed out where to sign and initial.

Laurence tried to hold still, but he needed to sign another paper. He glanced at the clock on the wall. The second hand didn't seem to move — except with the beat of Scott's pulse.

The pile of still unsigned papers was never-ending. This was taking forever! And this was a cash sale, it would have been worse if he had a mortgage attached to it. The great pounding of Scott's healthy heart held him spellbound. He felt so dehydrated, he wished he could have a little sip of blood.

Scott set the next paper down. "Are you okay?"

Laurence's head felt like it would explode.

"Laurence, are you okay?" the agent said a little louder.

He looked at Scott. Bloodlust took over his body.

His hands shaking, he took a sip of Betty's concoction. As the liquid flowed against his tongue, the tang of blood relaxed his frazzled nerves. It wasn't human, maybe a cat? He calmed. He took another sip. "Yes, sorry. Just a bit of a panic attack. Sorry."

"Don't worry. We're half-way there."

More papers. Minutes went by. Each time, he felt woozy, he took a drink and calmed. After a while, Laurence didn't even know what he was signing until he received his final copy of the closing disclosure, deed and the house keys.

He'd successfully bought his first home. He was a landed gentleman!

L AURENCE HURRIED UP THE PORCH AND knocked on the main floor of Betty's house. "Hi, Betty."

She looked at him through the door. "Come in."

"So, the closings all done. Thanks for the drink. It helped. How'd you know I'd need it?"

"Your friend gave it to me."

"What friend?" The room spun in front of his eyes. He leaned against the wall.

"Sit, before you fall," she ordered.

He sat on her couch.

"That girl who brought you home. She seemed like she was used to taking care of such things. Poor little thing."

"Yes, Norma is used to taking care of things," Laurence said softly.

"It's funny how I didn't remember her until two nights ago, but when I saw her knocking on your door, I knew it was she and her father who brought you home.

"She saw me and asked if you were home. Since you weren't, she said you'd need the drink for closing. There was no charge.

"I said I wouldn't give it to you unless she told me what it was.

123

"Norma explained she and you were vampires."

Laurence cringed.

"— which is why you sleep all day and work all night. The potion was to keep you awake and aware on the day of your closing. It's just cat blood, blueberry and spinach juices for vitamins and minerals."

Laurence expected her to be shocked, but she said this with the matter-of-factness of the elderly human at the end of her life who had seen everything.

"Betty..." He didn't know what he wanted to say. It was death for Betty to know of vampires. It was death for Norma to tell humans their secret.

She shrugged. "Takes all kinds. You pay the rent and are a respectful tenant. That's what matters."

"You're being calmer than I expected. Most humans don't react this way." He rubbed his hands on his jeans.

"I do have some questions."

"Please don't ask me to change you."

"I wasn't. I'm curious if it's more like *Interview with a Vampire* or *Twilight*?"

Laurence laughed. "I only skimmed *Twilight*, but we burn in the sun, not sparkle. Thank God for sunscreen."

"So more like *Interview with a Vampire* in that sense."

"It'd be more like *Interview with a Vampire* if we were all good-looking, rich French Lords turned Rockgods who could read minds. But I've never met a rich vampire."

"Even with lifetimes of compound interest?"

"It's hard for the undead to get mortgages or insurance through traditional means. Now there's all this shit with ICE. Some vampires don't have the correct paperwork even if they've lived here for decades. Sorry, I'm getting political...

"I've been saving money since the 1950's to be able to afford a house, and I told you how rundown it is. I mean, I love it, but it's definitely one of the worst houses on South Beacon Hill. I've been kicking myself for not purchasing a house in the 80's when prices were more reasonable.

"The only coven in Seattle is middle class, maybe a little better off because they own some property. The property which they live on is their biggest asset. They struggle all the time. Someone does something dumb, needs a couple thousand dollars to clean up the mess. Or worse, someone gets in a car accident and injures someone. Now they need half a million. In a coven, everyone chips in to help. If they are a loner like me, well, they make a decision to skip town or commit suicide before they are arrested and immolated their first day in jail."

"You don't make it sound appealing."

"It's why I don't drive."

Betty nodded and patted his leg. "Does that girl, Norma, live with her father?"

"They're business partners," he lied. Betty might be able to accept vampires, but reanimated corpses had a really bad rap due to all the flesh-eating zombie stereotypes. "Norma's the brain; Carlos's the brawn of their operation. She looks like a kid, but isn't really."

"I get she's not a kid, but he, Carlos, isn't the one who changed her, is he?"

Laurence realized Betty was concerned about Norma and didn't know how to ask her question without offending him.

"No. Vampire covens have rules, but they don't generally punish the victims, only rule breakers. When the coven found out what her maker did ... well, the coven..."

"Spit it out. You might live forever, but I won't," Betty said.

"Dismembered him and left his body parts to burn in the sunrise."

"You were part of that?"

"No, I'm not even a member. Norma was taken into the coven and cared for until she attended UW and started her own business."

"Oh, good, because I invited them for supper," Betty

said.

"Supper?"

"Yes. I thought I'd make you a nice steak to celebrate. Norma said you could eat meat as long as it was bloody. I'll be sorry to see you go, but so happy for you. Now, you let me know if you want more time to do some repairs. We'll work something out on a month-to-month basis."

"Thanks. I'll let you know by tonight about my move-out, and yes, I'd love a steak. What time?"

"Eight."

"Great, I'll be back around 7:30. I need to go to the house and do a few things there."

He hurried to the basement, grabbed the box of earth and called an Uber.

Careful to sit where the sun didn't hit him, he chatted with his driver, but his mind was on Norma. How much had she helped him?

She got him home; that much was clear. She helped him buy the house, helped him through closing.

He could send her a message, but maybe it didn't matter. If she wanted something from him, he'd soon know it. If the Paper Flower Consortium wanted something from him...

Maybe she was right; he was too paranoid.

Another block went by. He simply couldn't take it. He had to know. How did the old saying go? *Just because I'm paranoid doesn't mean you're not out to get me.* He texted Norma with the hope she felt his anger in the communication.

Why in the hell did you tell Betty I'm a vampire?

Dude. She's a smart lady, you don't think she noticed your fangs?

She might have evicted me!

No way. She said you're the best tenant she's had in years!

The coven might come after her.

This is serious!

Oh, shit. You're serious. Don't worry. The coven doesn't even know about her, but I marked her house, and I'll mark your new one next time I pass by. No one will mess with you.

Well, no one would mess with Norma, because everyone used her service.

I've been marked since I moved to Betty's house?

Not that long, but longer than you'd think. Once I found you, I didn't want to lose track of you again. If I'd known I'd have never left you there to rot. I would've come got you and brought you to a safe place.

I wouldn't have felt safe in the coven

No, shit. I wouldn't have brought
you there.

why?

why what?

Why are you helping/protecting me?

...

He saw the ellipsis, but he didn't wait for her reply.

I'll NEVER join your damn coven

P will be 😭💔 if something happened
to you. Besides I owe you

No. You don't. Leave me alone.

I don't want to owe PFC another debt
when your bean counters find me...

Stop typing and listen

I would've walked into the sun if you
hadn't told Agata and Jakub it was safe
to sleep in a bed and sometimes a
couch.

WTF?

I know. 500 years old and they didn't understand they didn't have to sleep in coffins. CRAZY!

Norma sent a gif of someone falling into a comfy-looking bed covered in white sheets. Laurence vaguely remembered the image from a fabric softener commercial.

TTYL. I'm going to Betty's tonight. Promise I'll tell you everything, but let me 🛏zzz

He tried to discern what Norma was referring to. It had been so easy to forget what Pascaline had said: ***Agata had to hold her to keep her in a coffin.***

How many days did Norma suffer lying awake in the coffin, next to a cold woman in death's embrace?

A strega needed a safe place to lay her head. She wasn't made through the standard program. No one sang at her rebirth or held her hand. For Norma, a safe place had never been a coffin. Or even the coven. She made herself a home somewhere in Seattle, someplace safe, unknown.

T HE UBER STOPPED IN FRONT OF LAURENCE'S new home. He thanked the driver and slipped out under his umbrella. His home's beauty made him breathless. Like him, this house would be immortal. Nothing could ever take it away from him.

Though he'd eventually paint over the pink and purple siding, for now, he found it charming. A sense of security washed over him as he turned his key in the loose lock, put his shoulder to the door, and stepped inside. He needed to get that fixed.

He inhaled the scent of his house. He smelled the grapefruit cleaner Karen used the day before, old wood, Formica, and cat pee.

"I really have to rip out that carpet as soon as possible," he said.

He slowly moved from room to room and prioritized renovations.

Since the living room's two small north-facing windows were a standard size, he'd go to Second Chance Center to see if he could find some panels of opaque stained glass. On the east wall, he'd place his television to watch the games. When he could afford it, he'd get a new couch and a larger TV.

The kitchen and bathroom's old Formica countertops would be changed to matching granite. While he didn't cook, granite was easy to scrape off and cool to the touch. The faucets worked. They could be changed later.

The bathroom sink might also need to be replaced. Maybe if he sold another painting or two, he could do more next year.

The appliances were twenty years old, but they could stay—except the washer and dryer as he wouldn't use them much anyway. The old laminate in the kitchen and bath would be replaced with tile which he had done before with Rob, and he could restore the old pine floorboards himself though it would take some time. The one thing he had in abundance was time.

Since the single bathroom sat between both bedrooms, Laurence decided that the smaller north-facing room would be his own. The other room would be a library with an overstuffed couch where he could read at his leisure. He could replace his TV with a big screen to watch the game in the living room, and, as Norma had suggested, his dining room would be his studio. He would add thicker curtains to make it seem normal and, behind the curtains, he'd cover the windows with wooden shutters on timers to block any daylight.

Even if someone accidentally opened a window, the small north bedroom was and would always be in complete shade. It was safe, but the smell of cat urine was overpowering. He lifted the carpet. Sweat pouring from his brow, he rolled it and pushed it into the hallway. The padding was crumbling underneath, but he folded it over to expose the old pine floor covered in dents and broken staples. He removed as much as he could without tools or a broom.

Think logically. Don't get too worked up about the budget.

"Refinish the bedroom floor first, get thick curtains, and interior shutters for the small north facing window. Then move out of Betty's. The dining room is in fine shape for my studio. Those are the two most important rooms."

Whatever he had left over, he'd start at the kitchen and bathroom. He'd restore the house room by room as the money came in. There would be problems. Even some that he didn't know yet. It didn't matter. This house would become as immortal as he.

He sprinkled his former homes' soil into the four corners of the bedroom and lay flat on the old pine floorboards. He set the alarm on his phone and shut his eyes to sleep the sleep of the dead. He was safe.

Laurence was home.

ABOUT THE AUTHOR

MUCH TO HER CHAGRIN, Elizabeth Guizzetti discovered she was not a cyborg and growing up to be an otter would be impractical, so began writing stories at age twelve. Three decades later, Guizzetti is an illustrator and author best known for her demon-poodle based comedy, ***Out for Souls & Cookies.*** She is also the creator of ***Faminelands*** and ***Lure*** and collaborated with authors on several projects including ***A is for Apex*** and ***The Prince of Artemis V.***

To explore a different aspect of her creativity, she writes science fiction and fantasy. Her debut novel, ***Other Systems***, was a 2015 Finalist for the Canopus Award for excellence in Interstellar Fiction. Her short work has appeared in anthologies such as ***Wee Folk and The Wise*** and ***Beyond the Hedge***. Between long projects, she works on a ten-part novella series, ***The Chronicles of the Martlet***, following the life of an elfin assassin turned necromancer just for funsies.

Guizzetti lives in Seattle with her husband and two dogs. When not writing or illustrating, she loves hiking and birdwatching.

To find out more about her work follow her on
Twitter @E_Guizzetti

ALSO BY ELIZABETH GUIZZETTI

Comics published by ZB Publications

Faminelands
Out For Souls&Cookies!
Lure

Fantasy published by ZB Publications

The Grove
Chronicles of the Martlet

Science Fiction published by 48Fourteen

Other Systems
The Light Side of the Moon

Illustrations published by Apocalypse Ink

A is for Apex
written by Jennifer Brozek

The Prince of Artemis V
written by Jennifer Brozek

CPSIA information can be obtained
at www.ICGtesting.com
Printed in the USA
FFHW022329091218
49768955-54249FF